**Other Matt Cobb Mysteries
by William L. DeAndrea**

Killed in Fringe Time

Killed on the Rocks

Killed in Paradise

Killed on the Ice

Killed with a Passion

Killed in the Act

Killed in the Ratings

# Killed in the Fog

## A Matt Cobb Mystery

**William L. DeAndrea**

**Simon & Schuster**

SIMON & SCHUSTER
Rockefeller Center
1230 Avenue of the Americas
New York, NY 10020

Designed by Jeanette Olender
Manufactured in the United States of America

10   9   8   7   6   5   4   3   2   1

Library of Congress Cataloging-in-Publication Data
DeAndrea, William L.
    Killed in the fog : a Matt Cobb mystery / William L. DeAndrea.
        p.      cm.
    1. Cobb, Matt (Fictitious character)—Fiction. 2. Americans—
Travel—England—Fiction. I. Title.
PS3554.E174K58    1996
813'.54—dc20                                    96-8453
                                                CIP

ISBN 0-684-83054-X

For Warren Murphy and Molly Cochran

# 1

**"Hello, good evening, and welcome . . ."**

David Frost
*The Frost Report,* ITV

/n the end, it turned out to be the biggest nest of nastiness I ever found myself exploring. When it was all over, Inspector Bristow told me that the whole thing had involved no fewer than thirty-seven separate crimes, though I have to admit that some of them, like "menacing" and "uttering false documents" were technicalities in the sense that the Major League (or as they say here, Premiere Division) evil could hardly have been carried on without them.

I wasn't left out, either. I'm down in the books as a victim—"Assault with Intent to Cause Grievous Bodily Harm."

I like the "intent" part of that. I was harmed, and I was suitably aggrieved by it, too, but cops everywhere like to go by the book.

It was a huge scandal, and it made the tabloids here go wild (more about them later), and I'm told it even made the media back in the States, hopelessly garbled, of course. But even the Brits never learned of more than a fraction of it. If you want to know what happened with TVStrato Satellite TV, and the death in the family Arking, you're going to need an American to walk you through it. I can do that. I was right there in the middle of it, from beginning to end.

Of course I was. How could I not be? It was exactly the kind of thing I moved to London to get away from.

Roxanne tells me it was Fate, with a capital F, but I blame the animals. I blame the animals because if I didn't, I would have to blame her, and that kind of thing is no good for a relationship.

Maybe I'd better put a capital R on that.

I mean, I have a relationship with the guy who delivers the milk (they still do that in London)—the relationship is friendly near-strangers.

But Roxanne and I have a Relationship. You couldn't say we rushed into it. We've known each other for years. I was working for the Network in New York when I met her. She was the grand-daughter of the founder of the Network, and she had run off with an extremely unsavory character who had her on drugs and on the street in that order.

I found her cowering in a tin-roofed shack not far from the railroad in Albany, New York. I took care of the unsavory character (talk about Grievous Bodily Harm) and brought Roxanne back to her family, such as it was, where she proceeded to beat the odds and astound cynical old me by straightening her life out completely without substituting something like an odd religion for it. She did, however, attend a succession of universities, accumulating an incredible number of degrees in different disciplines, before focusing in recent years on history, and actually turning out some prestigious publications.

Anyway, I'd known Roxanne for years before I'd admit, even to myself, that I was in love with her. I'm ten years older than she is, for one thing, and for another thing, with her grandfather and parents dead, she became the largest single stockholder in a major American corporation. In other words, Maj—Premiere Division Rich.

I was old-fashioned enough to let that bother me for a long time. I don't know why I came around. She didn't get any less younger than I am, and she certainly didn't get any poorer. Possibly, I finally got mature enough not to give a damn about what other people thought as long as I knew what the truth was.

All the time I'd known her, I'd had the same job—Vice President in Charge of Special Projects for the Network.

My, that sounds good, doesn't it? Gives you visions of arranging for coverage of presidential elections or the Olympic Games and stuff like that.

Wrong!

Special Projects at the Network in question was in fact a genius bit of euphemism. A "special project" was the housecleaning and coverup work any giant federally regulated industry needs. We handled everything too secret for security and too touchy for Public Relations.

It was interesting work, and challenging, too, but I got sick of it. Special Projects work carried the same occupational hazard as the one that faces cops and reporters and emergency-room workers—you're always dealing with people at their worst moments. It leads to cynicism.

That's not so bad. Cynicism can be fought. The real blow comes when you discover that cynicism is *right*. That any other attitude makes you vulnerable and ineffective.

I'd run into that wall about eight months ago, when I failed to spot something excruciatingly obvious and inadvertently let a killer run around and do a lot more mischief, all because I liked the guy.

When something like that happens, you have to take a long, hard look at what you're doing with your life. If I was going to go messing around in murders and similar nastiness as a full-time job, I'd have to be prepared for full-time cynicism. Call me selfish, call me a cockeyed optimist, I wasn't ready for that.

On the other hand, if I was serious about wanting to hang on to enough humanity not to feel like an idiot every time I found myself starting to like someone, I had no business doing what I was doing.

So I opted to get away. To say Roxanne was supportive of my decision was an understatement.

The conversation went like this:

ME: Rox, I think I'd better get away from the Net—

ROXANNE: I'm packed!

The next stop was at the Network headquarters on Sixth Avenue, in the penthouse office of Tom Falzet, president of the Network, and my on-the-job hair shirt for years.

Since our opinions of each other were reciprocal, you would have thought he would be glad to see the back of me, but no. He appealed to my loyalty. He offered me a raise. He claimed the Network couldn't live without me, which was ridiculous, since it had been in business the better part of fifty years before I ever came along.

He did everything, in fact, except throw me a testimonial dinner to show me how much I was loved.

It became apparent that I was never going to get the heck out of that office unless I gave a little on *something*. So I let him call my departure an "indefinite leave of absence" instead of a resignation.

Outside on Sixth Avenue, Roxanne kissed me and started waving for a taxi.

"You go to your apartment and start packing," she said. "I'll meet you in two hours?"

"What are you talking about? I thought we could go somewhere to celebrate."

"We can celebrate once we're packed."

"What is this packed stuff?" I demanded. "I thought that was just a figure of speech. Where are we going?"

"It was a figure of speech when I said it." The wind blew a tendril of long dark hair across her mouth. It was summer then, and she had a simple print dress on her small, round self, and she looked simply fabulous.

"You look fabulous," I said.

"Thank you, dear, you look yummy yourself, but let's stick to the subject. It's no longer a figure of speech, because we have to get out of town, preferably out of the country, and damn quick, too. I haven't decided where yet."

"Why?"

"Different requirements for visas, how much money my lawyers can get where, stuff like that."

"I don't mean *that*," I said. I was beginning to get a little breathless. Roxanne frequently has that effect on me, in all sorts of differing contexts. "Why the hell do we have to leave the country?"

She kissed me again and smiled. "Because you, Matt Cobb," she said, "are a Boy Scout."

"Would it be an imposition to ask you what the hell you're talking about?"

"Not at all," she said. She peered downtown. "No roof lights. God, it's murder trying to get a cab on Sixth this time of day, isn't it? What I'm talking about is your letting Tom Falzet talk you into a leave of absence, dear."

"I'm out, right? Isn't that what we wanted?"

"Oh, it's what we wanted, all right. You just have to remember that Falzet was the Network's top salesman for years before he became president. He's still a salesman at heart, and he's got you halfway to a sale already."

"I don't get it."

"Maybe not, but if we hang around, you will."

I worked hard to keep my voice from squeaking. "I will *what?*"

"Get it," she said. She went on, more helpfully. "Look. You're home from work, hanging around the apartment, walking the dog, watching TV, making love to me until your brains fall out . . ."

"So that's how it happens," I muttered.

She ignored me. ". . . in other words, everything that makes life worthwhile. Then the phone rings, and it's Falzet, and lo and behold—"

"Are they back together again?"

"You can laugh, but I'm imparting wisdom here. Lo and behold, there's a big-time Crisis at the Network, Communications as we know it is imperiled, and only one man can save the day, namely, you."

"That's silly," I said.

"Sure, it sounds silly the way I'm putting it now, but Falzet will give it the master salesman's touch, and you'll fall for it. Don't think you won't. You've got a hero complex. No. It's worse than that. You actually are a genuine hero."

"Come off it, Rox."

"You rescued me, didn't you?" She went on before I could answer. "Anyway, Falzet would *tell* you that it was just that one superspecial crisis, but as soon as you cleaned it up, he'd be around with, oh and as long as you're in the building you won't mind having a look at these other trifling problems, just take a few minutes of your time, and whammo! Before you know it, you're sitting behind the desk again, mistrusting your dog."

Jesus, I thought reverently, she's right again. That was exactly how it would happen. When a cab finally showed up, we got in it together, and I helped her pack.

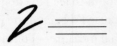

## "Walkies!"

Barbara Woodhouse
*Training Dogs the Woodhouse Way*, BBC

Somewhere down in the bowels of the house, I heard Roxanne say, "Millings, isn't it time to feed the dogs?"

"Yes, Miss Schick," Millings replied, "Oi shall attend to that doi-rectly."

Millings was a wiry guy, not so little, who looked after the dogs. He loved dogs, any kind, from racing greyhounds to useless lap-dogs like Pomeranians or shih tzus. He talked about them constantly in an accent Americans would call Cockney, but wasn't.

It wasn't because, "You see, Mr. Cobb, Oi did not 'appen to be born wivvin' the sound of Bow Bells. Oim a westerner, in fact, from doi-rectly across the Thames from 'ere in 'ammersmith." He had bright white hair, always combed flat to his head, no matter when you met him, bright blue eyes, and a bright red nose, which bespoke his major indulgence, namely the consumption of numerous pints of lager at the Oar and Megaphone, the local pub. I'm not going to transcribe his accent anymore.

Oh. As I found out to my peril, British pints are very big. Twenty ounces as opposed to sixteen. Over the course of what is universally known as "a few," this adds up.

In any case, when I heard Millings tell Roxanne that he was about to feed the dogs, I buried my head under my pillow. Not because I'd been done in the night before by the treachery of imperial measure—I'd learned my lesson about that the first time. Nor was it because I didn't want to hear the voices. Rox's voice is low, with a little raspy note to it, like Blythe Danner's, cute and sexy at the same time. To hear Millings is to be transported back to the pub scenes in the Basil Rathbone Sherlock Holmes movies, a world I love, though I admit he can get to be the teeniest bit grating sometimes.

No, gang, I buried my head under my pillow because I knew that when he brought the various foods out into the garden, the ten dogs quartered out there were going to bark as if no one had ever served them food before or ever would again.

Every morning and every evening, it sounded like a goddamn fox hunt out there. It was driving me nuts.

Then there were the cats. Five of them, kept inside the house. They were not vicious cats. They were cute cats, and a lot friendlier than most. They even played with Spot, my dog (more or less mine, anyway), a purebred Samoyed, who, along with the Roxanne Schick millions, was the proximate cause of all this.

These were swell cats. They didn't shed much, or eat horrible, smelly food and breathe on you. They came and sat in your lap, and tunneled their warm, fuzzy heads under your hand when they wanted to be petted, and just did cute kitty stuff until you wanted to sell them to a Chinese restaurant.

Because they *never stopped*. It got to the point where I was tempted to reach inside my pants and scratch my ass, not because it itched, but because I wanted once to reach for *something* and be reasonable sure of not getting hold of a wet little cat nose instead.

And you couldn't sell these cats to a Chinese restaurant, any-

William L. DeAndrea  14

way. These kitties were the spoiled darlings of Roxanne's society friends. Well, friends is a bit too strong a word. Rox has never had a lot of use for New York Society, and she undoubtedly burned that bridge irrevocably with her runaway episode as a teenager.

Still, as the granddaughter and heiress of most of the Network founder's dough, she was on a long list of charity sucker lists, some of which she actually contributed to. This kept her on speaking terms with her contemporaries and their mothers, who remained immersed in society stuff up to their tasteful diamond earrings.

And once it came out (God alone knows how these things get out) that dear little Roxanne Schick could get their snookum-ookum kitty-witties through that nasty British quarantine, all of a sudden Rox was the long-lost princess of the Four Hundred.

I think I'd better explain a little.

The first thing we had to decide after we decided we were skipping the country was what country we wanted to skip to.

I started by ruling out the Third World. The Third World is loaded with two things I absolutely cannot stand—poverty and hot weather.

I also ruled out any country where the citizens' major pastime was butchering each other for obscure reasons. This left out former Yugoslavia and Northern Ireland. We eliminated the rest of Ireland and a whole lot of other places because they harbor terrorists.

"If we keep this up," I said at one point, "we won't even be able to stay *here*."

"Don't be silly. We've got Australia, New Zealand, and all of Western Europe to go."

"What about Canada?"

She shook her head. "Too close. Falzet doesn't even have to dial zero-one-one to get to Canada."

"Well, I speak French, German, and Spanish."

"Spain would be too hot for you."

"How do you know?"

"New York's too hot for you."

"That's why God gave us air-conditioning."

"God hasn't given Europe air-conditioning to the same extent he's given it to us."

"How do they sleep?" I was half-kidding, but I still kind of wondered. I'm a cool-weather sleeper. Roxanne and I share a bed, but not a blanket. She wants an electric blanket at least, while I, winter and (air-conditioned) summer, am happy with a light comforter, or duvet (doo-vay) as they call them here.

"The thing is," Roxanne said, "you speak four languages fluently, whereas I speak one language. Lousily."

"You mean, no Belgium?"

"Not if we can avoid it, no."

"Shame," I told her. "I like the waffles."

"You haven't done much foreign traveling, have you, Matt?"

"Southeast Asia, courtesy of Uncle Sam, and St. David's Island, courtesy of the Network. I do have a passport."

"That's something."

"How about Scandinavia? It's cold, it's boring, and practically everybody speaks English."

"Boring?"

"In the sense of you don't see them on the news wiping each other out."

"Hmmm," she said. "Well, there *is* John Ericsson. . . ."

"And who," I asked, "is John Ericsson?"

"Was," she said. "He invented the Monitor. Maybe I could visit his hometown and do an article."

"Ah," I said. Roxanne, as I mentioned before, was making a little rep as a historian, and she was kind of focusing in on the Civil War. I'd better say the American Civil War. She had no job to lose, of course, so "publish or perish" didn't apply, but she did like to keep her name in front of her peers.

Now, you might think that after a hundred and thirty odd years of intense scrutiny Civil War scholarship might be about played out, and so did I, but that shows how little you know the Academic Mind, especially the History type. The thrust of Historical Scholarship as I perceive it secondhand, from hanging around Rox, is to keep the argument going at all costs, so that no question, however trivial, is ever settled completely.

What the heck. It makes her happy, and it keeps her off the streets.

But now we had a problem. My darling was hauling me off to Europe to keep me out of the clutches of the Big Bad Network, but if she could, she'd like it to be to a place where she could do *something* related to her own work.

"We seem," I said at last, "to be avoiding the obvious."

"What do you mean?"

"I mean we should go to England. I've always wanted to go there, anyway. I've read twelve million English mystery stories, from Miss Marple to Jack Regan, so I know it's not all country cottages and cutesy stuff like that."

"You'd want to? It seems so mundane."

"Excuse me, Miss Sophisticate, okay? I'm just a Manhattan boy from Yorkville who thinks it would be a swell place to go."

"Don't get me wrong, Matt. I'd like to go there myself."

"Well, why not? They speak English in England—speak it damn well, for a bunch of foreigners. It's cold, they've got color TV, and there must be tons of stuff about the Civil War. I know the South kept begging them to intervene."

"I've already thought of that," she said. "Plus, I own a house there."

"You own a house there," I said. Living with a rich girl can be a strange experience.

"Nothing incredible," she said. "Just five bedrooms. On the South side of the Thames, in Barnes. My grandfather bought it for my mother. She did a season in London. The estate has kept it up, modernized, but I haven't been there in years."

I forced myself to breathe slowly.

"Darling," I said, "if I were discussing flight to another country, trying to decide which foreign clime to sample, and I happened to own a house somewhere, I might have mentioned it more near the *beginning* of the conversation."

She looked at me in beautiful, round-eyed innocence.

"It slipped my mind," she said.

It slipped her mind. Once again, I had to remind myself that love had led me into a new world. Shortly after we moved in, the house next door, virtually identical to Roxanne's, sold for five hundred thousand pounds, or roughly three quarters of a million bucks. It slipped her mind.

"Anyway," she went on, "that's not important. If we did go to England, what would we do with the dog?"

Ah yes, the dog.

Specifically, Spot, a purebred, pure white Samoyed, a breed of Siberian sled dog with a cloud of fluffy white fur dotted with black eyes and nose and split with a perpetual black grin.

Spot and I had been together for some time now, but he was not, technically speaking, my dog. He was the property of Rick and Jane Sloan, college classmates of mine with family monies older and more voluminous even than Roxanne's. They had caught Archaeology the way my honey had caught History, only they did it the hard way, on their knees in sand or mud, patiently digging shards of pottery out of a grudging earth. The deal was, I would watch Spot and their Central Park West apartment while they were gone.

Well, I could easily arrange for security on the apartment, but what could I do about Spot?

Bring him? Well, yeah, of course, I wanted to bring him. It wasn't as easy as that.

You see, they have no rabies in England.

They have measles, mumps, chicken pox, and for all I know

phthisic and any number of diseases you never see in the States anymore, thanks to vaccination. They've got Slapped Cheek Disease (no, I never heard of it either, until I saw a case in the local supermarket and asked some questions; it's a form of measles that leaves the kids' faces bright, bright red, as if they'd just been enthusiastically slapped): and God knows what all else the National Health Service hasn't gotten around to vaccinating against.

But they have no rabies.

They got rid of it during the early years of the twentieth century by the simple expedient of killing every dog on the Island of Great Britain that had it—and every cat, squirrel, and dormouse, too.

They keep it out by a strict quarantine. Every animal, from elephant to whale to hamster, that is brought to this island spends six full months in quarantine. Even pampered animals such as Spot, who has had more shots than an L.A. gang war.

It's a tough policy, but a smart one, and a good one. Rabies is no joke, either for people or for animals. But how could I let them put my dog in the clink for six months? How much less could I let them put my friends' dog behind bars for six months just because I wanted to spend an extended time out of the country?

Well, I couldn't. I was about to tell Roxanne we were back at square one, when she pursed her lips off to one side, a sure sign that her gifted and unusual brain was clicking away.

"I know what to do," she said.

And she did, too.

It was something I never would have thought of, mainly because it took (a) an incredible amount of money, (b) some serious connections, and (c) the chutzpah that comes only with the habit of using both.

What she did was as simple and audacious as wiping out the rabid animals was in the first place. Roxanne got her house declared a quarantine center, or *centre*, as it says on all the forms. I said they speak our language darn well for foreigners, but not perfectly.

*Killed in the Fog*  **19**

Anyway, she pulled strings in the State Department and learned the requirements the Ministry of Agriculture set for quarantine centres and got contractors to build them. Somehow, she also goosed along a bunch of inspectors to inspect the place and get it approved, all within a month. (Yes, we stayed packed for a long time).

I never did ask how much it cost.

Anyway, came the Friday morning we were set to depart. The doorman rang up to my apartment, telling me the limo was there. The driver came up to help with the bags. I took Spot's lead, and we headed for the elevator.

As we were walking out the door, the phone started to ring. I started back to get it, but Roxanne stopped me.

"Leave it," she said. "It's Falzet. He's got some crisis at the Network."

We flew across on the Concorde. It was an amazing experience—two and a half hours across the Atlantic, no jet lag, a very quiet ride, because at supersonic speed you outrun the noise of the engines. First class all the way.

The only bad thing about the trip came when we commented to the British Airways stewardess (they still call them that) how pleasant the flight was.

"Thanks," she said, "mind you, they haven't made any new Concordes in twenty years, so this one is at least twenty years old, and nobody knows how long a Concorde lasts." She sighed. "It'll be a sad day when these come out of the fleet."

She went on talking about how great the plane was to work in, but we didn't hear her, because Roxanne and I were both working very hard at keeping the wings in place by staring at them.

We made it without incident. Spot loved the new place, and even though we couldn't take him out on the street, there was a fenced-in place in the back where he could walk around.

From the outside, Roxanne's house was not a beautiful place. It was big and square, of whitewashed brick, with a lot of lumps with windows in the middle of them. Inside, it was decorated in a lot of maroon velvet and dark wood. The furniture was overcarved and clunky, but it was also solid and comfortable.

I liked the place almost as much as Spot, and I got to sleep with the lady of the house, too.

Then the other animals started moving in, all of them, dogs and cats alike, during the first two weeks we were there. I looked up some statistics. Out of the fifty-five million people living in the United Kingdom of Great Britain and Northern Ireland, two hundred fifty thousand are Americans. Most of these are military personnel, a lot are employees of multinational corporations, some are married to British nationals, and some, like Roxanne and me, are just hanging out.

But the statistic that got me was that Roxanne had *ten acquaintances* who had pets they needed to get through British quarantine.

It boggles the mind. Or at least it boggled mine. Not only that, but it got on my nerves, too. Spot always excepted, the barking and mewing demands for affection drove me so nuts that I made my big mistake.

With the assistance of a busman, I went to visit one of the Network's operations in London.

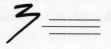

## "She who must be obeyed . . ."

Leo McKern (after H. Rider Haggard)
*Rumpole of the Bailey,* Thames TV

The Network had operations in London. European news was cleared through here, right off Trafalgar Square. Two floors down from that, there was a bunch of Network employees who attempted to sell Network shows in syndication throughout Europe and Asia.

I'd often wondered about the latter group. All the networks had them. I mean, it must be pretty simple to convince somebody that the special effects in *Star Trek: The Next Generation* are going to play in any language. But how do you persuade somebody to translate a static, line-driven sitcom like, say, *Full House* into Portuguese?

That was a question, however, that would have to wait for another time, because I didn't go there. I didn't go to Network News, either.

Instead, I went to the Network's newest and most grandiose London-based operation, TVStrato, a direct-to-home satellite TV service headquartered in London but serving all of Western Europe.

Mainly, it served them up a menu of recent movies, and sports (you paid a premium to have these channels decoded), along with a bunch of other stuff, including U.S. services like MTV and CNN, as well as more recent American stuff than you could get on the four British broadcasting channels.

We had it at the menagerie back in Barnes, and that was mostly what we watched. There's good stuff on English TV if you look for it, but when you turn on at random, you usually get one of three things—dramas wherein people in (and out of) eighteenth-century dress get laid a lot; sensitive documentaries on how cattle farmers on the drought-stricken Paphooda Peninsula in Upper Frammis deal with the ringworm infestations that have been plaguing their troubled economy; and game shows that feature borderline-retarded contestants having goo dumped on their heads by sadistic hosts.

It's nice to have the satellite—it serves the purpose cable serves at home. Not that they don't have cable here, mind you. A million homes were supposed to have been wired up by the end of 1994. Of course, considering that the population of London alone is something like ten million, I think it's safe to say that the satellite people will have it pretty much their way for the rest of the century, anyway.

TVStrato was not a wholly owned creature of the Network. If it had been, the name of it would undoubtedly have been something like NetSat or some other unpronounceable garbage.

With all the bureaucracy and (let's face it) anti-American paranoia rampant in these parts, the Network needed a European partner for this little venture, so they teamed up with British-International Communications, the media giant founded by the late Sir Richard Arking.

It was a short walk from the Hammersmith Bridge bus stop to

the ex–abandoned warehouse that had been gutted and refitted as TVStrato's transmission center and studios.

It wasn't a prepossessing sight, since no one had bothered to update the grimy Victorian exterior while they were at it, except for an incongruously brightly silvered sign over a new glass entryway. The sun glinted off it as I approached. From this distance, the various microwave towers and satellite dishes that had been built on the roof seemed like an infestation of particularly large and nasty bugs.

I walked in, and a young lady in a chroma-blue and gold TV-Strato page's uniform asked me my name and if I had an appointment. She was very pretty and blond and had nice teeth, and a little gold ball glinted from the left wing of her nose, just where the crease stopped on the way to its pert tip.

I pulled out my Network credentials—I was on an extended leave of absence, remember, so they were still good—told her I was over from New York and that I had dropped in on the chance I might get to see Bernard Levering.

"Certainly, Mr. Cobb," she said brightly. "I'll ring Mr. Levering's office straightaway. In the meantime, if I could just trouble you to step through the metal detector?"

I stepped, to a gratifying absence of beep. England doesn't harbor terrorists, but it is occasionally victimized by them. As a stockholder, I was delighted to see the Network and partners taking care of my property. As a creature of permeable membranes, spillable blood, and breakable bones who was at this moment in this building, I wanted to keep bombs out as much as anybody.

"He is?" the young woman in the security booth asked the phone at her ear. "Yes, that's right. Mr. Matt Cobb. Very good. Thank you."

She smiled at me again. She was very pretty. I tried not to stare at the thing in her nose until it occurred to me that if she didn't want people to look at it, she wouldn't have put it on display.

Of course, that logic could get you in trouble sometimes—it didn't seem to apply to low-cut dresses on either side of the Atlantic, for instance—but it seemed to hold me in good stead here.

"Mr. Levering will be right down to fetch you," she said. "Please have a seat in the meantime."

She waved me to a stark, modern, rectangular love seat in severe black leather and chrome. It was absolutely identical to the ones I'd left behind with Falzet on Sixth Avenue. I almost cried from nostalgia.

I managed to control myself. I sat on the love seat—it even felt the same—and wondered what people in offices do in that lengthy interval between the time someone tells you they'll be "out to fetch you straightway," and the time they actually show up. I wondered what I had done, when I had people showing up at my office, but I couldn't remember.

Eventually, Bernard showed up. The lobby directory here showed him as "Director of Operations," i.e., head of all the day-to-day business. He was a dark-haired, worried-looking little guy with glasses and an incipient stoop. He had worked for the Sales Department at the Network in New York for a couple of years before coming back to England to work for a then-budding TVStrato.

We'd gotten to know each other pretty well in those days. We hit it off. He'd become entranced with American sports, especially basketball, and I became his resident guru when someone leaked it to him that back in college I was a second-team small-college All-American. When I told him that in high school my best friend, next-door neighbor, and back-court partner had been NBA star Cornelius U. Martin III, he was ready to name a sneaker after me.

Anyway, Bernard soaked up knowledge like a sponge; learned that Bernard King pronounced his first name with the accent on the NARD, rather than saying Bernid, the way Mr. Levering and all his fellow Brits did; spouted statistics like three pages of agate in the *New York Post*.

And that was just basketball. It was the same thing with baseball and football, though without the hero worship.

I liked him a lot. He was quick-witted and funny, with a wry, throwaway delivery that never failed to crack me up.

Somebody once said we should try out for nightclubs as a transatlantic comedy team. Bernard replied, "No, I don't fancy us for the stage. We'd make a grand pair of hecklers, though."

"Matt," he said, pumping my hand enthusiastically in both of his. "Has New York sent you to check up on us, then?"

"No," I told him. "I'm here on holiday." That's what I told everybody. It was simpler than explaining that Roxanne Schick had so much damn money, the home office had given us visas that would let us stay in the United Kingdom until the next ice age, if we wanted to.

"That's great. How long are you going to be here, do you think?"

"Oh, another six months or so. Or until I figure out cricket."

"Another six months? How long have you been here already, Matt?"

"About three months. I think I've got rugby down, and snooker's easy enough to figure, but cricket is a challenge. I know Americans can do it, because an American owns the big cricket annual."

"Wisden's."

"Whatever. I've watched it assiduously, but all I can make of it is one guy working his head off, while the rest stand around not doing much of anything, and then it's teatime."

"Obviously," he said, "you're missing the subtleties."

I laughed. "Obviously," I said.

We went to a lift and got in. It was the same brushed stainless steel as in New York. I felt more nostalgia. I also felt that somebody's brother-in-law must have a racket going, selling elevators to the Network.

"Listen, Bernard," I said. "There's one more thing I don't understand about England."

"Just one? And after three months, too. My wife's been here for years, and she says she doesn't understand a goddamn thing about the place."

Now that he mentioned it, there were a lot of things I didn't understand, like how come when you bought the last of some item at the supermarket, they never ever restocked it, or why nobody would offer a discount on new books. But I let all that go for now, and addressed myself to the matter at hand. Or rather nose.

"What's with the downstairs receptionist?" I asked.

"Why? Are you on the outs with your ice skater?"

That had been two girlfriends ago. "We sort of slid apart," I reported, and Bernard laughed again.

"So you're interested," he said.

"Strictly academic," I told him. "I'm here with somebody."

"Oooh, 'er downstairs wouldn't like that. Judo-threw a guy from technical across the lobby and into a wall for stepping out on her."

"That must have gone over well with the management."

"You think you're being sarcastic, but as a matter of fact, it did. Her ladyship announced it was the first truly practical solution to sexual harassment she'd ever heard of. She gave the bloke the sack and Jill (that's her name) a pay rise."

"Which she then celebrated by buying a diamond to stick through her nose."

"Aha," he said, "squeamish, are we? How old were you before you learned not to argue with a woman over fashion?"

"It doesn't come up much," I said.

"Lucky man. My wife's an American—you knew Sandy in New York—and she looks at magazines from two countries and clucks her tongues over all of them. But then one day she'll tell me she absolutely must have an orange-and-green checked cashmere scarf, and there is no peace on earth until she gets it."

"But doesn't it *hurt?*"

"A little," he conceded. "But I'm doing quite well here. I can afford the odd scarf, you know."

"Not a scarf, the thing in the nose."

"Oh. Well, Sandy doesn't have one of those. Things, I mean, not noses."

"You're doing it to me again, Bernard."

"I've quite missed you, Matt," he said.

The lift stopped; we got off. Bernard introduced me to a couple of people who waved to me without looking up from computer screens, then led me to a nice mid-size office, tastefully furnished.

I took a seat while he got settled in behind a big, marble-topped desk. He liked marble for his desk top, he explained, because it was cooler when he went to sleep on it.

Right now, he leaned back in his swivel chair, cleaned his plain, black-framed National Health Service eyeglasses on the end of his tie and said, "Now, what do you want to talk about besides noses?"

"I'm not done yet."

"Ah," he said.

"I just get curious. I mean, it's not a cultural thing. Jill's face is as English as a box of Weetabix."

"Have you tried them?"

"I love 'em," I said. "I never saw anything get soggier faster and still taste good. But there are practical considerations. What if you wear one of those things and you get a cold? You must bruise the inside of your nose like fury trying to blow it."

"You seem to have given the matter some thought," Bernard said.

"You gave me plenty of time to consider it, and I had her nose in front of me the whole time. You ought to get some magazines down there. And what," I went back to the subject, "happens if you *do* get off a good blow? I can just see the thing going *ptweeng!* and there you are on your hands and knees combing the rug for an expensive piece of jewelry that just flew out of your nose."

I was warming to the subject. "And there's a clasp inside, right? So don't you think that snot must accumulate on it and—"

Just then, the door to Bernard's office burst in and a woman entered. In her own way, she was magnificent, at least as tall as my own six two, iron-gray hair, bright red dress clinging to a figure that was roughly cylindrical, except for a frontage that looked like a shelf waiting for a set of the *Encyclopaedia Britannica*.

I was raised right, so I would have gotten to my feet even if I hadn't jumped to them in surprise. Bernard did likewise.

"Hello, Lady Arking," he said. "How can I help you?"

She ignored him and turned a hawklike gaze on me. "Matt Cobb?"

"Yes, ma'am," I said.

"I consider your presence here an outrage, and I demand an explanation immediately!"

4 ═══

**". . . It's a simple matter.
He needs to express his
defiance."**

William Russell
*Callan,* London Weekend Television

I looked at her. My face was calm, but inside I was singing with joy. Oh, the freedom of not having to give a damn.

I was bland. I said, "You do, huh? Nice to meet you by the way. You must be Pam Arking."

I knew I should have said "Lady" Arking. You don't (I don't, at least) spend three months in a place without picking up at least that much of the quaint local customs. I left it off on purpose, to see what sort of reaction it would bring.

What I got was a hiss, in stereo. Behind me, Bernard sucked in breath, shocked at my temerity. In front of me, her ladyship was gathering air for an explosion.

I didn't let it go off.

"And you call me Matt, okay, Pam? I was a big admirer of your husband's, you know. Keep up the good work." Over my shoulder, I said, "Hey, Bernard, it's been great. We've got to have you and Sandy over to the house some time, as soon as we get rid of the livestock."

Puzzled looks. I hadn't gotten around to telling him that I was living in a quarantine house, or, for that matter, that I was sharing it with a woman who was her ladyship's only rival (along with Oprah Winfrey) among women in the communications industry for dough, if not for clout.

"Let's keep in touch," I told Bernard. "Nice to meet you, Pam."

I started for the door of Bernard's office.

"Mr. Cobb," Lady Arking said. It was a voice that could have stopped a charging rhino.

It stopped me. I turned and said, "What is it, honey? I'm in a hurry."

"I should like to see you in my office."

"You should?" I was sympathetic. "That's a shame. Because you see, I have a very important appointment with a person with manners."

I felt sorry for Bernard. He was gazing out his window with a look of desperation, as if he wanted either to turn into a pigeon and fly away from all this or jump to his death and escape it that way.

Lady Arking put on a show of her own. First, she went as gray as her hair, then as red as her dress. If she could do that on demand, she would be a natural as a halftime show for Ohio State.

She stared at me as if I were a bug under a microscope, but I'm used to the kind of look from Tom Falzet, so I just stared good-naturedly back.

She raised her eyebrows, and it was as if she'd hit some sort of switch—when they came back down, her face was a perfect blank.

Her voice, which had started rough and had been approaching downright raspiness smoothed out, too.

She said, "Of course. Mr. Cobb, if you could be so kind, won't you please join me in my office for a few moments?"

"I would be delighted to, Lady Arking. Since you put it that way."

"I," she said emphatically, "do." She turned to Bernard. "Please forgive me, Mr. Levering, for poaching your guest."

Bernard was sort of sickening. Yes, Lady Arking, he was leaving anyway, as you can see. No problem, at all, your ladyship. Take him, he's yours. He did everything but say he was sick of my face anyway.

It was a side of him I'd never seen in New York. I told myself not to be too hard on him. He was a young man with a wife and kids who probably wanted to go to Eton to hobnob with the nobs, and his nightmares probably all started with his losing this job.

I, on the other hand, was not only single, I had (a) a rich girl-friend and (b) money put aside, all on my own. In fact, at my insistence, I was paying half of all the expenses of our visit except for those concerning the extra beasts.

Heads did not exactly poke out of office doors and say "oooh" as Lady Arking strode regally down the corridors with me in tow, but there was a definite cessation of talk as we walked by.

There are lots of ways of being the boss, and you really can't argue with results. British International Communications made a lot of money for shareholders around the world, and Lady Arking had undoubtedly inherited the style as well as the business from the late Sir Richard.

In the unlikely event I ever took Roxanne up on her teasing offers to install me at the head of the Network, I suppose I'd insist on respect (admittedly a tough thing when everybody knows you hold your job solely because of whom you're sleeping with), but I would try to downplay the Awe and Silence bit. That sort of thing isn't even granted to the Queen anymore.

Lady Arking had a corner office overlooking the river. The same people who'd done the entrance had done this place, giving her a set of windows equal to the view. I could see barges on the Thames, and rowing eights, and Hammersmith Bridge. Across the river, I could see some of the rugby fields of St. Paul's School.

If I could see that, I might be able to see Menagerie Manor and blow Roxanne an unsuspected kiss. I looked, but there were too many trees in the way. Autumn is weird in London. There's hardly anything in the way of autumn leaves. The chestnut leaves turn yellow, and there's some good color from some kind of vine whose leaves are shaped like a maple's, but that's about it. For the rest of it, you say goodnight to a green tree, and wake up in the morning to a front yard (garden, they say here, even if the thing is buried under six inches of concrete and the only thing it ever grows is wet in a rainstorm) full of dead brown leaves.

It hadn't happened on the streets between the river and our address, so Roxanne's house remained invisible.

"Please sit down, Mr. Cobb," Lady Arking said.

"I will," I told her, "but only because you remembered to say 'please.'"

"It will probably help us move this conversation along, Mr. Cobb, if I inform you that I have no sense of humor."

Here, alone with me, she looked very tired. Still indomitable, but very tired. I felt sorry enough for her not to go on testing her sense of humor or lack thereof.

"Yes, ma'am," I said. "What can I do for you?"

"That you already know. I demanded it before; now I shall ask it civilly. Will you please explain to me how the Network's top investigator turns up at our joint venture and closets himself with one of my top executives without my very *knowledge,* let alone my consent?"

"Ah," I said.

"Ah, indeed. If there is any dissatisfaction with the way I have been running our joint venture, let it be expressed openly and aboveboard. This project was a dream of my late husband's, and to be frank, I have denied other BIC ventures my personal attentions until TVStrato was up and running profitably."

"Now, on the verge of achieving that—"

I could see that she was wound up for a long sermon, and since I wasn't the kind of sinner she was aiming at, I cut her off.

"Lady Arking," I said. "Lady Arking?"

*Killed in the Fog*

She was so into it, it took a few more repetitions before she realized she'd been interrupted. The knowledge irritated her.

"What?" she snapped.

"I think there's been a misunderstanding."

"There has been no misunderstanding of the joint venture agreement. Article Four explicitly states that I am to have day-to-day executive responsibility in all—"

"That's not the point."

"Then will you kindly get to the point? Please?"

"The point is," I explained, "that I'm not the Network's top investigator anymore. In fact, I'm not anything anymore. I'm not working for the Network."

"You used a Network credential at the downstairs desk," she said. If this were an episode of Perry Mason, I would crumble about now.

"I'm on a leave of absence," I said. I told her the whole story, except for the fact that it was Roxanne I was keeping company with. If she got this paranoid at my being in the building, the fact that the Network's biggest stockholder was with me would send her clean around the bend.

When I finished, she eyed me suspiciously.

"So you're here strictly on holiday?" she demanded.

"Came to the U.K. at Heathrow Airport early in August. Want to see my passport?"

"That won't be necessary," she said.

I guessed it wouldn't, at that. Woman with that much juice could have the flunky of a flunky call the Home Office and find out when I'd entered the country.

"So your visit to TVStrato was strictly coincidental."

"Right. I've been here for a few months, just settling in, acquiring a taste for pork pies, reading the *Times* and the tabloids when I finally realized I had an old friend living here I hadn't given so much as a phone call."

"Levering."

"Exactly. I knew him in New York; his wife once worked for the Network. I went to their wedding. I decided it was time to make contact, and since I'm living not too far away, a short ride on the number 69 bus, and it's a nice day, I further decided to call in person instead of phoning ahead."

She mulled it over for a few seconds. "I intend to check this information, Mr. Cobb."

"Dear lady, you may check my information until you are blue in the face. I don't give a damn, for I am telling the truth. So little do I care, in fact, that I am not even going to make one little phone call and tell New York that there really is something fishy going on around here."

Her voice was ominous. "I have told you I have no sense of humor, Mr. Cobb."

"Right. And therefore I wouldn't presume to joke. Item: You have security grassing to you instantly the second anybody walks through the door. There was no way you could have burst into Bernard's office so quickly with my name on your lips. Item: You're as tense as a piano wire, next thing to hysterical. Item: You are totally paranoid about your authority here and threat to it, to the point where you're sure you're being investigated by your partners, and to the point where you make dire threats about checking my story. Do you want more?"

Her voice was ice cold. "That will be all, Mr. Cobb. Good day."

## 5

**". . . I just want to see some action in my life."**

Theme song
*Dream Stuffing*, Channel Four

Three days later, Sunday afternoon, found Rox and me on Wardour Street, just where Chinatown meets Piccadilly Circus, stuffing ourselves at our favorite dim sum place. If you want to go out on Sunday, you have to leave Barnes, because aside from the Safeway supermarket on the Upper Richmond Road in nearby East Sheen, everything is closed, including a lot of the restaurants.

If you would like to know how a restaurant stays in business when it doesn't offer Sunday dinner, one of the major eat-out times (at least in the States), so would I.

It's frustrating, but this place we stumbled into one afternoon when we were just touristing around serves little plates of oriental ambrosia every day August Heaven sends, between twelve and three in the afternoon.

Rox and I had just finished demolishing various servings of paper shrimp, ginger beef, barbecue steam buns, sticky rice, spring rolls, fried wontons, and other delicacies, and I was reaching for my wallet.

I'd had such a great time at the meal, I forgot what else was in my pocket. As soon as I touched it, I frowned.

Roxanne picked up on it in a flash.

"You don't have to do this, you know."

"Yes, I do. I promised."

"I don't care. Besides, you didn't have to promise."

"You didn't say that at the time."

"I said it was up to you. It was up to you. I didn't say I'd be glad with your decision."

"Up to me," I scoffed. "What the hell kind of girlfriend are you, refusing to boss me around? They'll throw you out of the Guild."

She smiled. "I've never been much of a joiner," she said.

I smiled back. "Come on," I said. "You were as impressed as I was."

Roxanne bounced her head from side to side, loathe to admit it. At last she said, "Well, yeah. I mean, her ladyship dropping in on us. Incognito yet."

She was only wearing dark glasses and a scarf over her hair," I said. "I recognized her instantly."

Roxanne was exasperated. "Matt," she said, "the woman came in a *bus*. Not in a limousine, not in a taxi, not even in a minicab. In a *bus*." She shook her head. "Believe me," she said, "I grew up among people like this. If she had a heart attack, she'd spurn the ambulance and insist on being taken to the hospital in a limousine."

"She wasn't born to it, you know." I'd stopped in the Castelnau library in our neighborhood and done a little checking up. "Her parents were teachers, and she was a reporter on one of Sir Richard's regional papers, down in Brighton."

"Hove, actually," Roxanne said. "But that just strengthens my case. People born to big money just don't give a damn. People who marry it always feel as if they have to live up to something."

"I'll keep that in mind," I said.

She narrowed her eyes and looked at me for a long time. I figured my big mouth had gotten me in trouble again, and was already drafting several apologies based on what my offenses were likely to have been, when Roxanne said at last, "Is that a proposal?"

"I thought I more or less proposed last summer, and you more or less accepted."

"You're more or less right," she conceded. "I thought what you said right now might be a proposal to do something *about* it."

"Any time," I said. "You know that."

She pushed aside a few empty plates and took my hand. "I know, Cobb," she said tenderly. "And as soon as I can persuade you out of this macho nonsense about a prenuptial agreement, or as soon as I can stop taking it as a personal insult, we'll do the deed."

"I don't want it because of you," I said.

"Why then? Because of you? I think the idea of providing for the failure of a marriage before you even start it is sick."

"Look," I said. "There are three things people will believe about any man, and one of them is that he married his wife for her money. If we get married, they're going to think it about me—hell, they think it now."

"So what do you intend to do about it?" she demanded. "Hand out Xeroxes of your prenup every time you meet somebody new?"

"I don't intend to do anything about it."

"Then what's the *point*, Cobb?"

"The point is, when we walk into a room and people start to smirk, I want to know in my heart that they're wrong. I want to know for myself that I could, if I wanted to, prove that I'm with you because God sent you to earth to alternately make me ecstatic and drive me nuts."

She smiled in spite of herself. "Which is it this time?"

"Little of both."

"Well," she said. "I must admit you've come up with a new argument. Let me think about it."

"Sure," I said.

"But I tell you that coming in a bus for this woman was traveling incognito."

It took a few seconds to whip my brain back to the previous conversation, but I got there, and conceded the point.

Incognito or not, Lady Arking's visit was pretty bizarre. Rox and I had just finished dinner—lamb chops, peas, roast potatoes, choice of mint or red currant jelly. This had been prepared by the extremely soft hands of Miss Roxanne Schick her own personal self—we had a cleaning lady who came in, but no cook. God knows where Rox learned how to cook, but she's a natural at it. God knows she didn't learn by helping her mother, the way I did. Anyway, we take turns, cook together, or order out.

I was just loading the dishwasher when someone started plying the enormous brass doorknocker outside. There's a perfectly good doorbell out there, too, but nobody ever notices it.

The usual things happened with the clatter of the knocker. I jumped. Spot and the cats all ran for cover. Roxanne said, "Matt, get that, I'm not dressed."

Relatively prosperous and in London though we were, there was one aspect of what Americans perceive as British home life we were never going to adopt, and that was hanging around the house in smoking jackets and dresses.

When Roxanne said she wasn't dressed, she didn't just mean she wasn't dressed for dinner. She meant she was wearing a baby blue flannel nightgown over which she had one of my old plaid shirts from L.L. Bean.

I was wearing sweat pants and a T-shirt, but by some arcane feminine logic, this made me more prepared to answer the door than she was.

"Just a minute!" I yelled, as I always do, though considering the thickness of the oaken door, I'm sure nobody ever hears me.

It certainly never discourages them from crashing the goddamn door knocker down again. I start to feel like Errol Flynn barricaded inside a castle, with Basil Rathbone and a bunch of henchmen outside having at the door with a battering ram. I should be buckling on a sword, but instead, I merely step into a pair of moccasins (also from L.L. Bean) and one of my own plaid shirts if Rox has left me any.

Then I open the door to reveal an earnest person shaking a can at me, collecting money to fight the ringworm epidemic on the drought-stricken Paphooda Peninsula.

I had one hand on the doorknob and one reaching into the ashtray we kept on the small table by the door for some change.

The first thing I noticed was that the caller had no can. Then I saw who it was.

"Lady Arking?" I squeaked.

She winced and looked furtively around. I thought at first she might be overdoing things, but then I remembered that our neighbors on either side were a West End and TV actress and major solicitor from the City, and I reconsidered. Maybe I had been a little loud.

"Mr. Cobb," she said. She was nearly whispering, probably to set an example for me. "I know the intrusion is unpardonable, but may I come in?"

"Huh?" I said intelligently. "Oh. Sure. Of course." I stepped aside to make room for her, and she scooted in.

I waited a second as an old paranoid habit reasserted itself, and I took a quick look around the neighborhood to see if she was being followed.

The street was empty. I called myself an idiot and stepped inside. I took her coat and led her to what was called by British real estate agents the reception area but by me the living room.

And what to my wondering eyes should appear seated there but Roxanne Schick in a pert little green shirtwaist dress, stockings, and pumps, with a tasteful string of pearls around her neck. She looked as if she'd just come back from Sloane Square after tea with Di and Fergie and the rest of the girls.

She smiled at me sweetly, and suddenly I felt like a streaker. Great in bed, great cook, lightning-fast quick-change artist—

there was no end to Roxanne's talents. This from a woman whom I have personally seen take forty-five minutes to decide on a pair of earrings.

I smiled back, less sweetly. There wasn't much to do but brazen it out, then strangle my beloved at a better time.

"Lady Arking," I said, "this is Roxanne Schick, my, uh . . ."

"Fiancée," Rox provided. I could tell she had just decided to strangle me back.

Still, Rox managed to carry the ball where I would have been thrown for a loss.

"It's such a pleasure to meet you," Rox said sincerely. "I must tell you, I've been extremely impressed with you since before I knew who you were."

Lady Arking had taken off the shades and the scarf by now and, with the gray mane loose, looked a lot more like herself.

Not totally, however. There was a diffidence about her, an uncertainty that didn't suit her at all. This was a woman born to be imperial, not make a wan little smile and say she didn't quite understand.

"Well," Roxanne explained, "I was a little girl when Sir Richard died, but I know my grandfather had plans to try to take over BIC at the time. Then when he saw the job you were doing with the company, he said, 'Forget it, that broad's too tough to mess with.' I'm in awe of anyone too tough for my grandfather."

Lady Arking laughed with real humor and appreciation, but she was not cheered up, if you know what I mean.

Rox asked if her ladyship would be willing to risk tea made by an American, and she said she was, so Rox went off to see to it.

I sat there in my slob suit and waited for the woman to talk.

"Mr. Cobb," she said at last, "I must apologize. I did check your story, and you were telling the truth in every particular."

"Thank you," I said. "Apology accepted. What else did Tom Falzet say?"

"How do you know I spoke to Falzet?"

"You're used to dealing with people at the top," I said. "Besides, you weren't the slightest bit surprised when I introduced Roxanne. You must have been told she'd be here. I can't see anybody but Falzet giving that information out."

Just about then, Spot decided the door knocker was not some dogcatcher from hell, and crept out to make friends. He's good at that.

"What a beautiful dog!" Lady Arking said, which is what everybody says on seeing Spot. "May I pet him?"

"He'll be crushed if you don't," I said.

Spot closed his eyes and enjoyed it. Now the cats started creeping out. I explained the quarantine business. She said she thought that was a clever idea.

She was really taken with Spot. "Yes," she said, "you're a handsome fellow, aren't you? What's your name?"

Otherwise perfectly sane people are always asking Spot that, as though they expected him to answer. As usual, I filled in the awkward silence. "His name's Spot," I said, and then I had to explain how the Sloans had named him for the gigantic white spot that covered his entire body. She pretended to think that was clever.

Roxanne came back with some tea and some shortbread. I love shortbread. We had a nice little nosh and made small talk. Finally, I said, "Lady Arking, don't you think you ought to tell me the real reason you came here tonight?"

"You don't have to be brutal, Mr. Cobb."

"I don't mean to be," I said.

"No," she said, stroking a cat now, the gray Persian whose owner planned to bring it to a castle in Scotland. "I don't suppose you do. It's just that I am not used to being in the kind of situation I find myself in, and I don't like it. Having to ask a favor. I'm much more used to being in position to give commands."

I looked for a twinkle in her eye as she said that, and thought I found one. Could have been wishful thinking on my part, I suppose. "What's the favor?" I asked. Then I thought better of it and said, "No. Wait a minute. Before you tell me—us—anything, there's something I'd better say. I'm on a leave of absence from the Network, and Miss Schick, though she's the largest single stockholder, has managed with great difficulty to keep herself off the board of directors at the Network, so that's all right. But we're both stockholders, and we have a responsibility to ourselves and our fellow stockholders. If something is truly wrong at TVStrato, once you were to tell us about it, we'd have to pass the news back to New York."

Lady Arking nodded. "Of course. I would insist you do it, if that were the case."

"So?" I demanded. "Is it the case?"

"I don't know," she said.

"You've got to do better than that," I told her.

"I have noticed something . . . *odd* going on," she said. "My stepson Stephen brought it to my attention at first. But whether it concerns just me personally, or TVStrato as well, I cannot say. No one at work knows anything about this except Bernard Levering, and he knows only what I'm about to ask you to do, not why. I give you my word for this much. I am honestly convinced the odds are overwhelmingly in favor of the latter."

I sighed the sigh of a man who is facing the fact that it is easier to try to swim in quicksand than it is to try to fight it.

"What's the favor?" I said.

**"You're nicked, Sunshine."**

John Thaw
*The Sweeney*, Thames TV

*T*he favor turned out to be nothing much. I was supposed to hand an envelope to an African man, about twenty-four years old, who would be standing in the queue outside Planet Hollywood, which happened to be just down the block from the Chinese restaurant in which Roxanne and I now sat belching with pleasure.

Having finally come out with the Big Request, Lady Arking spent the next ten minutes or so buttering me up, using the very finest English butter.

Not only, according to her, did I have a virtually godlike reputation at the Network, but the New York Police Department lost many management man hours repining the fact that such an honest and brilliant personage as I had not decided to become a cop.

That was the kind of person she *needed*, you see. Someone she could trust implicitly, yet whose name wouldn't be connected with hers by the curious or worse. Someone whose resourcefulness and discretion were beyond question.

And so on. It got to be embarrassing, and it was a mighty let-down when the task for which this paragon was needed was the simple delivery of an envelope. Still, with the butter laid on so thick (and the fantastic fact of her arrival on our doorstep to prove that whatever was going on here, it was desperately important to her), I decided to go along.

She took a sip of Roxanne's tea and pronounced it quite good. She took another sip. I could see her muscles loosen as the tension drained from her.

I got the particulars of my mission. They were simple enough. About 2 P.M. I was to be walking along Wardour Street in Piccadilly, where the line curves around the corner to get into Planet Hollywood.

There is always a line to get into Planet Hollywood. The one in London is part of a chain—they have a couple in the States, too—that's partially owned by a bunch of movie stars.

Now, working for the Network, I've met a lot of celebrities and I haven't gotten over being starstruck yet, so it would be understandable, it seems to me, to stand in line if Sly were going to bring you to your table, or Bruce was tending bar, or Arnie would sit down and jaw with you for a few minutes before Demi brought you the bill charging you six pounds (about nine bucks) for your hamburger.

But the stars haven't been anywhere near the place since the grand opening. These people (to be fair, they're mostly tourists, a lot of them Americans, who, if you ask me, ought to know better) wait in line every day for the privilege of eating a hamburger that costs nine bucks.

If Lady Arking's favor had called for *me* to stand in line out there, I would have refused on principle. As it was, I simply had to find the guy, bump into him, make us both drop our envelopes, then bend over and pick up his.

It was Amateur Night in Dixie, but I'd already signed on to play and it was too late to change the script. I considered pointing out that the whole thing could have been handled more efficiently by the Royal Mail (which delivers twice a day, by the way, U.S. Postal Service take note) for the cost of a pair of twenty-nine-pence stamps. I decided against it on the grounds that it wouldn't do anybody, least of all me, any good, and would make Lady Arking so nervous she'd move in with us.

After numerous reassurances on our part and thank yous on hers, we finally got her out the door. I wish we could have sent a couple of the cats home with her.

So now, I was moving in on my quarry. He was easy enough to spot. He was a six-foot-four-inch black man wearing a red, gold, black, and green dashiki and a round cap to match. His name was Joseph Aliou, and he was from Cameroon. Lady Arking had told me that, even though I had begged her not to.

I hustled down the street, pretending I was late for something or other. Aliou made it easy for me by standing on the edge of the pavement, practically in the street. I was heading downhill with a good head of steam, and I gave him a good, solid nudge. Basically, I wanted to make sure he dropped his goddamn envelope, which I did not see anywhere.

I did better than that, I practically knocked him off his feet. And of course, I nearly forgot to drop *my* envelope.

I let go of it in time, though, and I saw something flutter out from under his dashiki.

There were some comments from the crowd, including some imputing racist motives to my "assault."

Great, I thought. TVStrato was doing fine, thanks, but most of Lady Arking's money in the UK came from a sensationalist tabloid called *The Orbit.* I could just see the headline now: YANK AGITATOR IN PICCADILLY RACE RIOT SHOCK HORROR.

I instantly became Contrition personified, helping him steady himself, picking up the envelopes and carefully giving him the wrong (that is the right) one, brushing him off, and apologizing constantly, trying very hard to give the impression that I would have to be specially told before I even noticed the guy was black.

He, in the meantime, was Human Brotherhood, forgiving me even more quickly that I could apologize, his musical African-French accent soothing the rumblers in the crowd. It even made me feel better.

The exchange made, I gave him one last "sorry" and was on my way.

Five seconds later, someone shot him.

This was real-life gunfire as opposed to TV gunfire—short, sharp pops that didn't sound dangerous at all. I turned my head toward the sound just in time to see Joseph Aliou leak blood from a couple of places in his chest and begin to sink to the street.

My head spun around and I just caught a glimpse of Rox ducking into a stone doorway. Smart lady. She'd be okay. I looked back around—there'd been no more shooting, and most of the would-be burger buyers still had no idea what was going on.

I started to make my way through the crowd to see if I could help Aliou, but two things made me stop.

One thing was that plenty of people were attending him. One person had whipped out a portable phone (listen, rubbish collectors in London have portable phones) and was already calling 999 for help.

The other thing was that as I was trying to make my way *in* toward the victim, I saw somebody trying to make his way out. He was a short, light-skinned black man, maybe twenty to twenty-five years old. He was wearing Air Jordans, black chinos, a Chicago Black Hawks shirt under an L.A. Raiders jacket, topped by a Florida Marlins cap. It was a bizarre combination, but it was the fashion among lots of London youth to wear what they called American sports kit. Most don't even know which team plays what—they just like the designs.

What I *didn't* like was the way he was elbowing his way through the crowd trying to get to open sidewalk. That is, he was using one elbow, and one free hand to shove people out of the way.

The other hand was tucked firmly into the jacket pocket, holding something ominously heavy.

"Hey!" I said, and he started to run.

Sometimes I'm an idiot. It's dumb to startle someone you think has a gun in his pocket, a gun he had moments before used to strike down a fellow human being. It's a lot dumber than that to start chasing him when he runs away.

I did it, though. He dashed around the corner and headed along the two short blocks to Piccadilly Circus itself. I followed, with cries of "There he goes!" in fifteen different accents echoing after me.

Running along that stretch of London street was like trying to run through a hedge or a bamboo forest. The pavement was thick with people trying to get into Rock Circus or the London Pavilion to play video games.

It was supposed to be off-season for tourists, but you couldn't prove it that afternoon on that street.

I almost caught him six times, but he was small, shifty, and ruthless, and he kept eluding me, mostly by knocking people over. I didn't actually deck anybody, but running in his wake, I didn't have to—they were still down when I got there.

It was obvious where he was trying to go—to the end of the block and the entrance to the Underground. The Piccadilly Circus tube stop is such an incredible rabbit warren, once he got in there there'd be no catching him.

Miraculously, seven feet of open space appeared between him and me. With a spin move worthy of Michael Jordan, I got around a pensioner and closed the gap. I was going to catch him.

I was as close as that. I had my right arm raised to grab him by the shoulder.

Then something hit me, low and hard in the back of the knees, wrapped around my legs. I went halfway down the stairs on my chest and chin.

I got up ready to slug the SOB who'd tackled me and let the killer get away. I stopped the fist in mid-flight.

The helmet was askew and showed bright yellow hair. They eyes were blue and determined. The truncheon stood ready.

"Right," the bobby said. "You're under arrest for murder. Anything you say will be taken down and may be used in evidence."

**7**

**"So this is the famous
Scotland Yard."**

John Lennon
*Help!*, EMI Films

*H*aving been arrested from time to time in the past, in two different countries, I've picked up a few pointers.

First of all, don't panic. Most cops, even in big cities, go through life without ever arresting anybody for a felony. It's possible that the cop is more nervous than you are. He'll get in trouble if he overreacts to your nervousness and shoots you or beats in your head, but by the time he's punished for it, you could be well past caring.

Secondly, don't explain yourself. He's not listening anyway. He's making sure he gets the wording of the warning right, watching you for an excuse to shoot or beat your head in, or daydreaming about the wording of his commendation. He (or she, I don't want to be sexist, here) doesn't want to hear, "But, Officer, you're making a big mistake." For one thing, the cop involved doesn't think she (or he) is making a mistake. For another thing, if they have stepped in it, there's no way to wipe it off now, so they might as well tromp on. Yes, I know that while PC Nigel Staines (he showed me his warrant card after he slapped the cuffs, quaintly called "nippers," on me) was processing me for a ride to the local nick, the real killer was zooming away on the London Underground, but that battle was lost the moment Staines knocked me down the stairs.

Of course, in this instance, another reason for me not to explain anything was that I didn't understand anything. The only theory that made any sense at all to me at the moment was that Lady Arking had gone to a lot of trouble to frame me for murder, and that seemed unlikely.

Which brings me to a third thing to avoid. Whatever you do, do not evoke the names of powerful friends. It irks the cops, and rightly so. It can make them spiteful. They've busted you; they'll investigate you. They'll find out about your powerful friends soon enough and will be more impressed for the delay.

This was a subordinate reason for my not mentioning Lady Arking. The main one, however, was the fact that I wanted to ask her ladyship a few questions of my own before I turned the cops loose on her. At that point, in fact, as I was led to one of London's really hideous police cars (white, blue, and Day-Glo orange and magenta, nicknamed a "panda"—don't ask me), asking Pammy baby a few questions was my chief desire in life.

The fourth thing to avoid is uttering anything you'll regret later, like "Well, you got me," or, "It's a fair cop, guv."

Fifth, you've got to keep innocent outsiders from gumming up the works. Roxanne Schick was now showing her style at crowd-elbowing, bearing down on the police car with fire in her eyes. I caught her gaze and gave her a rapid shake of my head.

Sixth and last, what you *do* say is, "Yes, gentlemen, I'll make no trouble for you, and I wish to talk to my solicitor as soon as possible."

You can say this as many times as you like, but you must say

*Killed in the Fog* **51**

nothing else, aside from giving your name and address and asking if you can use the bathroom. In this case, I said it really loud, so that Roxanne would hear me, and would get the solicitor thing in motion.

It was a quiet trip to the station. I was locked in a caged back seat with insufficient leg and headroom, and PC Staines concentrated on his driving.

I soon learned one of the disadvantages of living in a foreign country. Back in the States, Roxanne would have had Vincent Bugliosi awaiting my arrival on the steps of the police station. As it was, I had to wait.

And wait. I was booked in and printed. I had my belt, money, passport, and shoelaces taken away from me. I got to keep a receipt. I was taken to an interrogation room that was an awful lot like a lot of interrogation rooms in the States, right down to the phony one-way mirror.

The locked me in and left me alone. Maybe they expected me to walk up to the mirror, rub my chin and say, "Gee, who would ever believe that's the face of a man who shot down another man in cold blood just an hour and a half ago?"

If they were hoping for that, I didn't oblige them. I did stand up to pace a few times, but that was a huge dissatisfaction, since my sneakers flopped on my feet and my pants fell down every time I tried it.

The chair was hard and uncomfortable—there was no other chair, when they finally got around to interrogating me, they'd have to bring their own—I thought of sitting on the floor, but I figured they'd read something psychological into that. This case was complicated enough without bringing shrinks into it.

After about an hour, somebody popped in and offered me a cup of tea, which I accepted. It was good. An hour and forty minutes after that they popped in and offered me pizza.

They'd taken my watch, but I was born with this innate sense that always lets me know what time it is within ten minutes or so. When we first moved in together, Roxanne would wake me up from a sound sleep to test me. I was messed up for a few days after we flew to London, but whatever it is soon adjusted. Roxanne probably still thinks it's a trick, but it's not. It's what you call a mixed blessing.

On the one hand, you virtually never burn the rice. On the other hand you can lose a lot of sleep to skeptical girlfriends.

Another drawback is that when you're sitting in an ugly little room with only a phony mirror for company, you are aware of every second as it drags on by.

Another hour and a half, and despite my huge lunch, despite the stuff they put on pizzas in England (sweet corn? olives with pits? mashed potatoes? all of those, and worse), I was beginning to regret not having had a slice.

It wasn't too long after that, though, that somebody came into the room. He was in shirtsleeves and tie. He was almost as tall as I am, but thinner. He was in his forties, I guessed, with a crinkly face and dark hair that he parted low and combed sideways to cover a bald spot. He was carrying a chair that looked a lot nicer than the one I was sitting on.

Holding on to my pants, I rose to greet him.

He didn't offer to shake hands, but he did smile at me and tell me to sit down. He plopped his chair down and sat himself.

"Hello, Mr. Cobb, is it?"

"That's right," I said.

"I am Detective Inspector Fred Bristow. Sorry to have kept you waiting so long, but you understand we must have time to investigate so that we have intelligent questions to ask you?"

"Sure," I said. "I understand. Just the way I need to talk to my solicitor before I answer any questions. And I'm awfully sorry about that. It's been hours. I would have bet anything that he would be here by now."

*Killed in the Fog* **53**

"Have you had a chance to phone?"

We were both being so damnably civilized, I could barely stand it. Hypocritical, too. At least he was. He knew damn well I hadn't had a chance to call anybody.

"I'll just wait until he arrives," I said.

"As you wish. Do you mind if I talk to you for a while?"

I couldn't stop him if I did mind. I gestured graciously for him to go ahead. I might learn something.

"The man you shot was Joseph Aliou. Did you have a reason for shooting him?"

"You know, Inspector," I said, "I'll bet you have a million questions, and I'll bet I've got an answer for every one of them. But not till after I speak to my solicitor."

So he stopped asking me questions. Instead he stated some of the case against me, then raised an eyebrow as if to say, what do you think of that?

"We have a dozen witnesses who say you assaulted Aliou just seconds before he was shot."

Of course, if I'd been talking, I could have pointed out that "assaulted" was a loaded word undoubtedly put into the witnesses' mouths by the investigators. I could also point out that he had no witnesses at all that actually saw me shoot anybody.

"You shot him, then, when you heard one of the bystanders say, 'There he is,' you knew you'd been identified, and you ran. You ditched the gun somewhere before Constable Staines caught up to you. We'll find it."

I had to give him this much—he was good. He was leaving lots of good holes for me to jump into, trying to get me to start talking. I was literally aching to tell him that if he found it or didn't, it was no skin off my American ass, since something as simple as a paraffin test would show I hadn't so much as set off a Guy Fawkes Day firework.

"When your solicitor gets here," he said, "perhaps you'd like to explain why an envelope found in the dead man's hand has your fingerprints on it, and the one you were carrying had his."

I conceded it was possible.

"You might also prevail upon him to let you explain why the one he had contained postal money orders payable to bearer in the total of five thousand pounds, and why the one you carried contained a broacher for the B. E. Peters School of English."

"A what?" I said.

"A broacher. A flyer. An information sheet."

"Ah," I said. Actually, I knew all along he was trying to say *brochure*, and failing the same way all his countrymen did, but I thought I'd gain at least a little control of the situation.

Call it revenge. I am not a patient person by nature. I'm the kind of person who keeps burning his hand on the side of the slow cooker because I can't actually see or hear it doing anything. I have to, as my mother put it, command patience; I don't have a lot naturally. Sometimes I have to be quite stern with it. Sometimes, I have to squeeze my brain like an empty toothpaste tube in order to find some.

There was a war of nerves going on, and my only sensible strategy called for my not firing a shot. It was, not to put too fine a point on it, a bitch. I didn't even want to let him see me grit my teeth.

Finally, he left. Only about fifteen minutes went by before somebody got let in to see me. He was compact, blond, brisk, and businesslike, and somehow, he made me feel better just to look at him.

He handed me his card—Thomas David Williams, Solicitor, and the name and address of a big firm. That was about as Welsh a name as you could get, and the voice backed it up, with the rolling, drumlike cadences of that principality.

"Well then," he said. "Let's get down to business."

"Suits me."

"However did you get in this mess?"

"Let me ask you a couple of questions first, okay?"

"Sure."

"Are our communications privileged?"

"They are. Why do you ask?"

"I wanted to know," I said. "I never expected to get in trouble with the law here, and I didn't check."

"Yes, the privilege is absolute, just like in America."

"Good. You're likely to hear a lot more that way." I suddenly realized how tired I was. I yawned and stretched and said, "What took you so long?"

This brought a grim chuckle. "I haven't been quite as long as that, you know. The bastards kept me cooling my heels outside for a good ninety minutes. They seem quite upset with you. They're afraid this is a race killing and there are going to be riots. They'd like to hand you over on a platter to quiet them down."

"It wasn't a race murder," I said. "At least not the kind they're thinking of. The real killer was black."

"I think they'll be delighted to hear that, if you can back it up."

"Bunch of people must have seen me chasing the other guy," I mused, "but try to find them now."

Thomas David Williams said, "Ah," and pulled out a notebook. "You were chasing the real killer, then. That's why you were running from the scene of the crime."

"Yes, I was trying to do my duty as a good visitor with an extended visa."

"Yes, independent means. The lovely Miss Schick was telling me. The kind of visitor the nation likes most to have. If they can avoid getting into trouble, that is."

"Mmmm," I said. "How is Roxanne?"

"Worried about you. And angry. Ready to take Scotland Yard apart brick by brick with her bare hands if she doesn't get satisfaction. That was another reason my arrival was delayed."

"What else? Did somebody try to get to you?"

"Get to me?"

"Try to keep you off the case?"

"No. Why should they?"

"I don't know. I've been sitting here developing hemorrhoids on this rotten chair while the world outside has gone on spinning." Then I thought of something. "Hey, you're my solicitor, right?"

"I have been so engaged, yes." I didn't blame him for the note of caution in his voice—my face must have looked pretty maniacal by that point.

"You're supposed to look out for me and take care of me, right?"

"Well . . . within the law, yes."

"Don't worry, this is perfectly legal. Switch seats with me, okay?"

Williams looked dubious, but he got up and circled the table. I did likewise, then sat. The cushioned bottom of the chair brightened my whole outlook.

"So," I said. "What *did* keep you?"

"Well, it is Sunday afternoon, you know. I was with my family at our weekend place in Essex when Sir Bascombe rang me on the phone."

"And you had to drive in."

"That's right, and the traffic was a nightmare, I can tell you."

I believed him. I personally wouldn't drive in this country on a bet, even aside from the fact that they drive on the wrong side of the road. For one thing, this isn't that big an island, and there are too many cars on it. Like my native Manhattan, but not as bad. For another thing—and this is the clincher—gas costs about three bucks a gallon.

"Why you?" I asked. "There must have been someone in town."

Williams smiled for the first time.

"Listen, boyo," he said, just to throw a little extra Welshness on me, "I'm the major crime specialist of our firm. I'm very good at it. Not that I care for it much, mind you. I'd much rather be doing contracts and property and other nice, clean pursuits. But this is a prestigious firm, and when I go out on my own someday, it will look good for me to have been there. Everybody else at the firm went to public schools, and half their fathers worked for Tomlinson, Swath, Tomlinson, Sweggar & Peach before them. I went to a council school, and my father worked in a bloody coal mine. Do you understand me?"

"Better than you think," I told him. "Story sounds kind of familiar, as a matter of fact."

"You?"

"More or less. The actual notes are different, but the chords are the same."

"It can't be exactly the same. You can't break the class system in Britain, but you can bend it until it creaks, and that's what I intend to do."

"And God bless you in your endeavors. Who's Sir Bascombe?"

"Sir Bascombe Tomlinson. The second Tomlinson in the name of the firm. Brother of the first. Senior surviving member."

"I'm impressed," I said. "I didn't think even Roxanne had enough juice in this country to roust a knight—knight or baronet?"

"Knight. Sir Bascombe is quite active in charities. Law reform, widows and orphans, homes for aged and retired foxhounds, things like that."

"I'm impressed that even she was able to roust someone like him—I remember him now from the *Times*—on a Sunday afternoon."

"Oh, it wasn't just her."

"No?"

"No, indeed. Your lovely friend descended on Sir Bascombe's Sunday dinner in Sloane Square unannounced and in the company of no less a personage than Pamela, Lady Arking."

"Lady Arking," I said, not sure if I liked it.

"She is a major client of the firm," Williams said. "Of course, I have never had any personal dealings with her."

"Wait awhile," I said.

"I'm sorry?"

"Williams, who are you working for?"

"That can be interpreted as a very offensive question, Mr. Cobb."

"I don't mean it to be. I'd just like to hear your answer."

"I am employed by Tomlinson, Swath, Tomlinson, Sweggar & Peach. My fee, as I understand it, is to be paid by Miss Schick. But my client first, last, and always, is you." He stared at me. "Unless you desire some other arrangement."

"Nah," I said. "I like you fine. I'm just warning you, you may be starting your own firm sooner than you think."

I dumped the bag for him, all of it, from the time I walked through the door of TVStrato to the time PC Staines rode me like a luge down the stairway to the tube.

"Sweet Jesus," he said when I was done.

"My sentiments exactly," I told him. "Now how about getting the cops to give me a paraffin test and get me the hell out of here?"

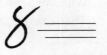

**"Now it's your turn in
the Spotlight Round."**

Noel Edmunds
*Telly Addicts*, BBC

*O*f course, it wasn't as easy as that.

In fact, it was so much less easy than that that it turned out to be impossible.

The first thing I decided was to keep Lady Arking out of it for the time being. Williams immediately proved that he meant that stuff about my being the one and only client by informing me I was nuts.

"I think you're carrying chivalry a little too far, my friend," he told me. "If you were to inform them about Lady Arking's connection in this matter—"

"Connection?" I protested. "She's the whole thing!"

"That just emphasizes my point further. If you want to get out of this cell, that is the quickest way. They'll flock to her like bees to the queen, and they'll bring you with them to confront her.

"Right. And she calls me a dirty, rotten liar, and I go into a dungeon for a hundred years."

"I won't let that happen," he said. He thought about it for a few seconds. "Not for a *hundred* years," he added.

"Yeah," I said. "I was exaggerating, but you get the idea."

"You don't want to mention her, then."

"No. Let's save her ladyship for some time when we've got enough leverage to make it stick."

"All right," he said. "This isn't going to please our friends in blue—"

"They're big boys now. Or should I say boyos?"

"Stick to saying boys and leave the music-hall taffy to me, hey? Mind you, tell them no lies. If we have to reveal all we know, any lie told now will make things worse."

"'A truth that's told with bad intent,'" I quoted, "'beats any lie you can invent.'"

He favored me with another of his rare smiles. "Brilliant, man. You have put your finger on the whole set of the practice of the law."

Williams went to the hallway and called the cops.

It was Bristow again. He saw us, excused himself, and came back with another chair. It wasn't as good as the one I'd appropriated, but he didn't try to get it back.

"Right!" he said briskly, as if encouraged to be under way at last. "So you're ready to tell your story, then?"

And I did, with every word *strictly true.* Not *copiously* true, I'll admit, but there wasn't a lie in the lot.

The way I told it, my fiancée and I had just finished lunch and were going to go up to Shaftesbury Avenue to get a bus back across the river, when I felt a sudden urge for a copy of the Sunday *Telegraph,* having already read the *Times* at home.

"You only like Tory papers, then," Bristow observed.

Williams was irritable. "What does that matter?" he demanded.

"Well, if this does turn out to be a racially motivated crime . . ."

"It would be more likely to have been committed by someone

who reads a Tory paper? Try that one in court. I can't wait until the columnists—even the ones on the *Guardian*—get hold of that idea."

They took a few minutes to thrash that one out, but it blew over. I went on with my story. I was on my way to see if the newsstand around the corner from Planet Hollywood was open (and I was, too; it was as good an excuse as any to go barreling into somebody, and I did want the paper—strictly true) when I collided with the man who was shot.

"Joseph Aliou."

"Right. Joseph Aliou. I bumped into him quite hard. We both happened to have envelopes on us—"

Bristow's face lit up as if he'd accomplished something.

"So now you admit you had the envelope with the five grand with you?"

I suppressed a grin. London cops were a lot like their New York brothers in a number of ways, but in this way, they were identical. To them, there is no such thing as an innocent fact. If you tell a cop the sky is blue, you have just "admitted" that, and will be held responsible for the knowledge. They never notice, it's not even worth calling to their attention, just a reflection of the world in which they live. I wouldn't have been surprised if DI Bristow went home and helped his daughter with her homework saying, "Now look, you already admit that six times four is twenty-four . . ."

So I admitted that I admitted it.

"Sure," I admitted. "I've never denied it. As you say, it has my fingerprints on it."

"Perhaps you want to tell me why you had the five thousand pounds in post office money orders, payable to the bearer?"

"You can't get any actual money bigger than a fifty-pound note," I told him, strictly true. "It makes a terrible bulge in large quantities." Also strictly true.

"Yes, but why were you carrying that much money in an envelope, in any form?"

"There is no law against it," Williams said. "Is there, DI Bristow?"

Grudgingly, Bristow admitted there was not.

"Eccentricity," I said, "sheer eccentricity." This was also strictly true. It was merely Lady Arking's eccentricity I was talking about.

Bristow was less than ecstatic with that explanation. He smelled a rat and jumped on it like a terrier and worried it for a few minutes, but eventually let it go.

I went on with my story; how I took a couple of steps by, then heard the shots, and chased the guy in the mixed sports regalia until I was collared by the long blue arm of PC Staines.

"That was a little foolhardy, wasn't it?" Bristow demanded.

"What was? Oh, chasing an armed man? Well, yeah. But I wasn't too worried, because before he actually started running he zipped up the pocket of his jacket. I figured even if he stopped and tried to get it out I'd have a chance to jump him."

Bristow raised his eyebrows clear up to his bald pate. The corners of his mouth came down, and he nodded, mock-impressed. "Oh, you noticed that, did you?"

"Yeah," I said, fighting a patience mutiny. "Someone had just been shot, and I was paying attention."

"Mr. Cobb," said Williams portentously, "has law enforcement experience."

This time, Bristow's surprise was real. "You do?"

"Yeah," I said again. "Years ago. U.S. Army. Military Police. Bangkok. Drugs, rape, prostitution, fights, gambling. The kind of trouble soldiers get into."

"I suppose your army records are available?" Bristow asked.

"I never heard of a bureaucracy ever throwing anything out."

Williams cleared his throat. "Ah, Mr. Cobb is being modest. Several times, he has helped the New York Police Department in homicide investigations."

"I suppose this is checkable as well?"

I sighed. Obviously, Rox had given Williams an earful. Still, the one person in the world a cop will trust is another cop, so let them check away. My credit balance with the NYPD and Detective Lieutenant Cornelius U. Martin Jr. was quite good.

"Very good," Bristow said. His mask of good nature was slipping, too. "Evidently, Mr. Cobb, you are quite a remarkable character."

"I'm just trying to get by," I said.

"Yes. Well, you may rest assured—and you, too, Williams—that everything Mr. Cobb has said will be checked down to the ground. In the meantime, sir, perhaps you might like to offer and explanation as to why five witnesses identified you as the killer. Or were they all eccentrics?"

"Not eccentrics," I said. "Just normal, scared witnesses. I collided with Aliou just before he was shot; that impressed me on a lot of minds. Then, after the black guy in the sports kit shot him, they saw me running. I'll make you a bet," I said.

"We do not gamble here," Bristow said.

I waved it away. "Just an expression. I will state something I believe to be true: you don't have a single reliable witness who can swear I had a gun in my hand. And no one who mentioned the slightest sign of recognition between Aliou and me, let alone hostility."

"So?" Bristow was well on the road to surliness by now, and that told me I was right.

Calculated risk. Witnesses can say they've seen any damn thing they can imagine, and cops have been known to plant the odd idea in a person's head, inadvertently or otherwise. I was glad that the Yard had held to such impeccable standards of questioning.

"So," I said, "one would think that if I was mad enough at this guy to kill him in a crowd on a Sunday afternoon, that he would be afraid, or angry or something. Wouldn't one?"

"Stop that," Bristow said, getting to his feet. "You sound like the Queen. We'll talk again in the morning."

He made as if to walk out. Williams filed briefs, appeals, demurrers, and all sorts of legal stuff, and concluded by informing DI Bristow that his client was insisting on a paraffin test, which would prove I hadn't fired a gun.

"Yeah," I said. "Nobody saw or found any gloves, either, did they?"

Bristow scratched his head, and knocked the carefully glued-down hairs awry. He then magically restored them in place with a sweep of his hand. Must get a lot of practice, I thought.

"Oh my, yes," he said. "I must be getting old. Clean slipped my mind, that did. Technician's right in the building, too. I'll go tell him to get ready, and somebody will be round to fetch you straightaway."

After he left, Williams and I looked at each other.

"What the hell was that all about?" I asked.

"From the way you told your story, I thought you had all the answers."

"What's that supposed to mean?"

"Every word, strictly true, as promised, but you've come mighty close to the edge. When we come to the end of this, and the whole story comes out, Bristow is not going to be your friend."

"That depends," I said.

"On what?"

"On what else I'm able to tell him at the time."

"Like what?"

"How do I know like what? Aliou was shot for a reason and not because the shooter didn't like the color of his dashiki."

"And you're going to find out why?"

"Let's just say I'm going to get Lady Arking tête-à-tête and take it from there."

"Cobb, this isn't New York, you know, where the cop is a second father to you. This is an away match, and the killer and who or whatever is behind him has a decided home-ground advantage."

"I know that. Maybe he was testing us."

"What?"

"Bristow. Maybe he refrained from mentioning the test to see if we'd ask for it. Obviously, if I were guilty, I'd try to avoid the thing like a stale crumpet. The longer we went without mentioning it, the more convinced he got that I was blowing smoke at him."

"Perhaps you're right." Williams bit his lip. "You're sure this test is going to show what you want it to show?"

"Don't you start on me now, Williams. Believe me, if I were going to kill somebody in this town, I'd do a lot better job of it than this."

He shrugged. "I told you this was an away match."

I didn't have to say anything to that, because somebody came along and fetched us.

I shuffled along the corridor in laceless shoes, holding my pants up, as a young Asian PC led us to a room very like the one I'd spent the last hours in, only a little bigger, a lot cleaner, and much better lit.

There was a little guy in a tweed jacket and a bow tie. He could have walked out of a 1930s Agatha Christie mystery. He introduced himself as Mr. Braintree, and he was the technician.

I responded as though I gave a damn what his name was. The English are tigers for introducing themselves. By this point, I was hungry, exhausted, pissed off, and a bit scared. I wanted food and a shower, and I wanted to crawl into bed with Roxanne and her teddy bear and sleep for a week.

Braintree spoke with a slight Scots burr, and he went about his business, setting out a bottle, some wooden swabs, and several plastic bags.

As he snapped on a pair of rubber gloves, he said, "We should have done this earlier. The sooner the better, or you can lose your opportunity."

"It wasn't my idea to delay it," I said.

"Well, you can't fight budget cuts, I suppose. Have you been to the toilet since the alleged shots were fired?"

I appreciated the word. There was nothing alleged about the shots; they happened all right. But I appreciated somebody trying to introduce some doubt into these proceedings.

"No," I said, "I haven't, and now that you mention it . . ."

"Please wait just a little longer, Mr. Cobb, if you will. Haven't washed your hands for any reason?"

"Nope," I said. "Haven't had the chance."

"Or wet your hands in any way?"

"No?"

"Then things should be fine, then." He smiled. "Left hand, please."

I gave it to him. He took it by the wrist, then opened the brown bottle.

"This," he said, "is a mild solution of nitric acid. If there are gunpowder residues on you hands, this will dissolve them, and they will be picked up on the swab."

He rubbed the swab all over my hand, but he concentrated on the area around my first two fingers and thumb, and the webbing in between.

"I understand you asked for a 'paraffin' test. If you'd been dealing with someone much younger than DI Bristow, you might have caused a bit of confusion. What you Americans call paraffin hasn't been used for this sort of test for many years, and here in Britain, paraffin is what you call kerosene. Other hand please."

He'd put the swab in a Ziploc bag and labeled it with my name, the date, and "lh-fngrs." Now he did the same to the other hand, and put that swab into a bag of its own. After that, he did the same thing to both palms and bagged and labeled those.

He spoke to the PC who'd been guarding me.

"I'll have the results first thing in the morning," he said. "Tell Mr. Bristow I'll ring him." With that, he bid us good evening and left.

And it soon became apparent I was going to spend the night in the cell, a first for me. I was not pleased.

*Killed in the Fog* **67**

Williams fought like mad, but there were no judges to appeal to, no one to set bail. No clear evidence of my innocence until the paraff—excuse me, nitric-acid test came through.

I asked, and was given, permission to use a toilet for humans before I got locked up. I gave my hands and face a good washing, too.

Williams said he'd see me in the morning.

I said, "Sure," and resigned myself to my fate. I wished I had a harmonica. Or a cake with a file in it. I wanted to see Roxanne one more time.

I had worked myself up to quite a pitch of self-pity; after that, the cell itself was an enormous letdown.

It had a door with a grillwork window, and there were walls between me and the other prisoners, mostly drunks and pickpockets. The place was meant for two, but I had no cellmate. The bunk was clean.

I could survive here through the night, if it was just one night.

Of course, it shouldn't have been any nights, and I got madder and madder thinking about it, especially when I heard my fellow inmates making foggy-brained speculation about what a high-priced American hit man like me was doing in the smoke shooting down coons from Africa in the first place.

Then I got it, and I started to laugh. I went to the grille in the door and shouted for the guard.

"Quiet now," he said. "It's late."

"Bristow," I said. "Is he still around? I want to see Bristow."

"What for?" The guard was suspicious. I wasn't surprised. I don't think that was the kind of job that inspired a lot of trust. Could make you cynical. Might make you want to take off to a foreign country with your girlfriend.

I was still laughing at that when Bristow showed up. He overruled the guard's suspicions, had himself let in, and sat on the other bunk.

"I'm on my way home," he told me. "Do you want to confess or something?"

"You know I don't," I said.

"I do, do I?"

"Yes," I said. "You do. You know it better than you know your own father's name. If you *do* know your own father's name."

"Watch it, Cobb," he said.

"Oh, get stuffed. I'm sick of you. I finally figured out why I'm in here."

"You're assisting in our enquiries."

"You're throwing the foreigner to the wolves."

"What wolves?"

"The press. Especially the tabloid press. The *Sun.* The *Star.* The *Mirror.* The *Orbit.*" It wouldn't have done to leave that one out. "You're writing their headlines for them."

Bristow did the hair trick again.

"I'm a cop, not a journalist."

"You're something," I conceded. "I couldn't understand why the famous Scotland Yard was being so weird. A sensational murder with a racial angle, and all of a sudden you've got all the time in the world. I had to beg for the test that would clear me. I had to sit on my ass for three hours before anybody even bothered to talk to me. It wasn't incompetence, it was deliberate."

"Now, why would I do a thing like that?"

"Like I said, you're writing headlines. If you'd brought me in and run the test right away, the results would be in now, and I'd be sleeping in my own bed.

"The only trouble with that was if you did it that way, the papers tomorrow would read POLICE BAFFLED BY PLANET HOLLYWOOD RACE MURDER SHOCK HORROR. Now, because of careful planning on your part, it'll be YANK YUPPIE HELD IN RACE MURDER. How nice for you. Even when you let me go—as you inevitably will have to, you'll do it in such a way as to intimate you'll nail me when you get enough evidence, the lack of which is only temporary. Meanwhile, I'll have to prove I'm not a murderer."

"You could always," he said, "leave the country. There'd be

nothing to stop you. That is, in the, um, unlikely event we had to let you go."

"No, thanks. I've got an extended visa, and I like it here." I looked at him. I'd never seen such a deadpan. "But forget about me for a minute. Don't you even give a shit about catching the real murderer? Who I almost caught for you, until PC Staines showed his rugger skills? If manipulating the press is all you care about, get out of police work and into PR."

And at last I got a reaction from him. His face came to life so quickly and so intensely that I jumped.

"Now you listen to me, you smug bastard," he said in a harsh whisper. "This city is a powder keg, like Los Angeles a few years ago, or a Detroit or Newark in the sixties. We've got militants, and we've even got a bloody Nazi holding public office. We've got teenagers who kill black boys for dating white girls.

"Now, I was born in London, and I live here, and I love it, and I would prefer not to see large portions of it go up in flames, while slaughter rages in the streets. I admit nothing, but I tell you that any racial incident, even something a lot less final than a murder, could set it off.

"Again, I admit nothing. But if it takes inconveniencing one rich American boy to keep that from happening, I might just be willing to do that, wouldn't I? I might even," he added, "do a lot worse."

I looked at him for a long moment, then clapped my hands, slowly. "That was truly beautiful, Bristow. Honestly, I'm touched. A man among men, that's what you are."

"You can save the sarcasm, Cobb. It doesn't make me laugh, and it doesn't do you any good."

"My heart bleeds. Listen, if you'd thought like a cop instead of a goddamn politician, you would already have checked me out with the NYPD and—"

"What makes you think I didn't?"

"You didn't. You avoided anything that would clear me before the papers went to bed. I hope to hell you're at least looking for the real killer."

"We've been looking for the man you chased," he said, as thought the admission caused him physical pain. "We got good descriptions from witnesses."

"Well, thank Christ for that. You're not a total loss. But look, if you'd called New York, you would have eventually gotten hooked up to Lieutenant Martin."

"And?"

"And he would have told you that you could still run your scam. I'd have played along with it. I don't especially care for riots myself, okay? And you could have been using your brain to smoke out the real killer."

Bristow scratched his jaw. His tongue worked in his mouth. He wasn't buying much of this, if any, but at least I'd created a seed of doubt in his mind.

Finally, he said, "You might as well get some sleep, Cobb. I've got some phone calls to make. I'll call you in the morning."

He left. I got rid of my laceless shoes and lay down on the bed. I went to sleep with the other inmates murmuring about how much time the DI had spent with the American Gangster.

# 9

**"Extraordinary crimes against the People, or the State, must be handled by agents extraordinary."**

Opening blurb
*The Avengers,* ITV

*S*o the test came back negative, and they let me out of jail about eleven-thirty Monday morning, just too late to make the earliest editions of the *Evening Standard,* London's last remaining P.M. paper.

Roxanne, I must say, did it up. I was met at the door of the nick by a chauffeur-driven Rolls Royce, and Roxanne dressed past the nines, all the way to the elevens, in a backless, strapless silver lamé evening gown. There was a lot of lovely flesh showing, but a not a goose bump visible, although it was a chilly morning, as most London November mornings are.

She clicked up the stairs toward me on silver high heels, with a magnum of Moët & Chandon in one hand and a crystal glass in the other. She got to me, smiled, kissed me, poured champagne, took one red-lipped sip, then held the glass for me. It was cool and good.

All of this was devoured eagerly by news photographers. Despite the overcast sky, we could have gotten a tan from flashbulb lights. I was beginning to understand why celebrities wore dark glasses.

I had my shoelaces and belt back, so I was feeling pretty terrific. A photographer yelled, "Kiss her again," so I did, at length. It should only have made him as happy as it made me.

"Hello there," I told her when we came up for air.

"Hello," she said. "I figured if they were going to make a media circus out of this, I'd give them a real center ring attraction."

"Papers bad?"

"Horrible," she said. "I've got them in the car."

"I can hardly wait."

As we made our way to the car, I just hoped Bristow was getting a good look at this out a window somewhere.

The hacks weren't going to be content with just pictures. Questions came at us rapid-fire.

"How was your night in jail?"

"I give it one sixty-fourth of a star."

"What are you going to do now?"

"Get on with my life."

"Is it true you've been completely cleared?"

"Ask DI Bristow. That's what he told me."

We fought our way through the hacks toward the car. The driver had come around to open the door for us. He was fending off the vultures with one arm.

I could have told him it wasn't strictly necessary. Possibly in reaction to the tension and devious game-playing of the night before, I found the more or less honest vulgarity of this whole process to be kind of refreshing.

"How do you feel about England?"

"Love it," I said.

"What about the police?"

"What about them? Human beings doing their jobs. It was an honest mistake," I lied.

"No hard feelings?"

"I just hope they catch the real guy." We'd reached the car at last. "Now if you'll excuse us . . . ?"

But they never do excuse you. More questions came flying out of the crowd. We could pick one out above the din, a skeptical, "Not bitter at all, then?"

Roxanne answered that one.

"Not a bit," she said. "He's sweet clear through."

We were laughing hysterically as we collapsed into the car.

"Home, James," I said.

"Very good, sir," he replied.

"Your name is really James?"

"No, sir, actually it's Nigel, but Americans like to call me James for some reason."

I laughed and turned to the papers. They were bad, just about what I'd expected, except there was more "shock" and "horror" thrown around than I had expected.

Lady Arking's *Orbit,* having had a head start in its partnership with the Network, had an exclusive on the "Strange Background of the Mystery American," which made me look like a combination of Sam Spade and Captain America. It had details on all the cases I'd ever been involved in, and, whether I had anything to do with working them out or not, managed to give me credit for them, including the case I'd screwed up so badly it drove me out of America in the first place.

It occurred to me that Bristow didn't even have to spring for the phone call to get a glowing recommendation of me—all he had to do was wait for the morning papers.

He had made the call, of course. He brought me a message from Lieutenant Martin: "What the hell have you gotten yourself into this time?" I'd let him know as soon as I had it figured out myself.

Another thing that occurred to me was that as big a pain in the ass as it was for me, Bristow's strategy had been a brilliant success.

None of the papers played up the race angle; they were too dazzled by the idea of an American gunslinger slinging said gun on the streets of London.

Tomorrow, unless DI GETS HANGNAIL SHOCK HORROR turned up, they'd be full of what an eccentric but fun guy I was, trading badinage with the press, with my rich and gorgeous fiancée at my side.

As the car got closer and closer to the South Bank of the Thames, I became less and less aware of the inanities of the papers, and more and more aware of just how gorgeous my fiancée was.

By the time James/Nigel had dropped us off at home, I was hornier than a triceratops.

Just inside the door, we stopped and kissed, an even better one than we'd done for the photographers.

Her dark eyes glittered. "Upstairs," she suggested.

"You little mind reader, you," I said, and picked her up and carried her. I dropped her on the bed, and she giggled as she bounced.

I joined her, and held her tight, kissing her neck and shoulders and the tops of her breasts. Then I found the zipper, and the gown came away like the shell of a hard-boiled egg. Progress after that was rapid.

After a long time, we lay beside each other.

"Wow," I said.

She twisted a finger in my hair. "Yeah, wow."

A little while later, she started to laugh.

"What's so funny?"

"You'd better stay out of trouble, Cobb, for both our sakes."

I told her that believe it or not, I always tried to stay out of trouble.

"Yeah, well do a better job of it. Cobb, you were only in jail for *one lousy night,* and look at us. What would we have done if you were getting out of jail after a week? Or a year?"

"Mmmm," I said. "Spontaneous combustion, at least."

Just then, the phone gave a short, quick double ring. That was good timing on its part. Ten minutes ago, I would have torn it out of the wall.

Roxanne picked up and answered. She said yes a couple of times, then, "Just a minute." She put her hand over the mouthpiece and turned to me. "Lady Arking's personal private secretary," she said.

"Sounds redundant to me."

"As opposed to her private business secretary," Rox explained.

"Oh." Rox never seemed to have anything to do with this kind of stuff, but she always knew all about it. Something genetic. I wondered, if we ever had kids together, if they could do this social stuff, too.

"Lady Arking would be pleased to have us for tea this afternoon. Sixish. She apologizes for the short notice, and hopes we'll understand.

"This is good," I pronounced. "Tell her we'll be there."

Rox did and hung up the phone.

"So we've got an engagement. I guess we ought to leave here about quarter after five. It'll be rush-hour traffic, but we don't want to be too early."

"No," I agreed. "I wouldn't mind if her ladyship had to sweat a little bit."

"But that leaves us hours to kill in the meantime," she said.

"I know."

"How are we going to pass the time?"

"Easy," I said. "We stock up."

"Stock up?"

"Yeah. In case I have to go back to prison some day."

I reached for her.

By six, it was already dark (actually, at this time of year in London, by four-thirty it's already dark), and after the cab let us off in front of Lady Arking's place in Regent's Park, backed on the canal and close to the zoo, we stood in the light of a streetlamp while Rox-anne made sure my tie was straight and I had both cuff links.

Since we'd gotten to Britain, Roxanne had been using me as a paper doll, buying me sweaters (they said jumpers) of Scottish wool and weird casual pants with pleats and only one back pocket, and all sorts of things she thought would look good on me.

It was nice to have an excuse to get back into the sort of outfit I knew I looked good in—conservative three-piece suit, navy blue wool with a discreet white pinstripe, white shirt, dark red tie with tasteful blue and gold stripes aimed down across my chest to my left hand.

I used to wear some modification of this outfit every day to work. I used to think of it as my Clark Kent outfit; Roxanne said I looked like a banker.

"You say that as if it were a *bad* thing," I told her.

"I've known bankers," she said ominously.

She herself looked terrific, as usual. In this case, she was wear-ing a dark blue shirtwaist with her dark hair drawn back in a loose ponytail held by a silver thing, plus silver hoops for earrings.

It was a pleasure to look at her, and while I was, I became aware of something. She didn't look so much like a little girl to me any-more. She didn't look *old* or anything, just more mature, more womanly. Maybe she was maturing before my very eyes. Maybe, after all these years, I was finally seeing her the way she really was. Maybe it was a defensive illusion on my part—when you are hav-ing sex with someone on a regular basis, only a sicko wants to think of that person as in any way a child. After all, she was twenty-seven by now, I was a little surprised to realize.

Whatever it was, it made me happy.

"Presentable?" I said.

"You look great," she said. "For a banker."

We walked up the eight steps to the door. I stood there for a mo-ment, looking around.

"What's the matter?" Roxanne demanded.

"Nothing," I said."I'm just making sure there's no doorbell be-fore I go crashing any doorknockers around."

There was no bell, so crash I did, with a clatter of metal into metal-over-wood that resounded through the park and brought jungle screams from the zoo.

It was interesting to learn that the sound of the knocker was just as obnoxious on the outside as it was on the inside. I decided to wait fifteen seconds, then let her rip again—I owed Lady Arking at least one more jolt.

I didn't get the chance; the door was opened in just eleven sec-onds. However, my disappointment at that was overwhelmed in my delight at seeing something I had never before seen in my life.

It was a butler, a real live butler. In livery.

And liver spots, too, on his veiny hands and on his bald pate. He must have been about a hundred and two years old, but then where do you find butlers in this day and age?

We told him our business, and, after looking disappointed that we didn't have any coats for him to hang up, he told us in a sur-prisingly strong voice that he would inform Lady Arking of our arrival.

I looked around the room he asked us to wait in, saw the por-traits on the walls, the chandeliers, the flocked wallpaper, the whole number, and I started to laugh.

"Share the joke?" Roxanne invited.

"We found it!" I said. "Millions of Americans come here every year looking for it. They tour the Tower of London, Buckingham Palace, Windsor Castle, but they never catch up with it."

"Catch up with what?"

"Christieland! Most Americans come to England expecting to find high tea, whatever that is, and village fetes, and vicarages and rose-covered cottages and stuff like that."

"We've seen all of that since we've been here," Rox protested.

"We've even met the vicar. He kept hinting about how happy he'd be to marry us."

"Yeah," I remembered. "Considering the unwed-motherhood rate in this country, I suppose he was looking to foreigners to save his job." He had even kept it up when he found out that I'm RC and Rox is Jewish, saying, "Nobody's perfect."

"Sure," I went on, "we've seen all that stuff, but it was either pasted on specifically for tourists, or it was, I don't know, fossilized. The main thing I remember from the Barnes fete was the rap music. That and the Indian food. I didn't get the Christieland feeling from that."

"But you do from here?"

"Yeah, I do. We stepped through that door into a kind of perennial 1937, it feels like. I don't know how Lady Arking leaves it every day to enter the real world, then comes back here at night. It must be worse than jet lag."

"I never knew you had this nostalgia Jones."

"I don't. That's the irony of it. I like modern London just swell. I was just thinking of all the people who came here and go home disappointed that they haven't seen the famous London fog."

Roxanne grinned. "I've been kind of disappointed in that myself."

"Me too," I admitted. "A little. But this house is the architectural equivalent of an old-fashioned London fog. Can't you feel it?"

"Maybe," she said. "And maybe Bambridge is going to come and get us and lead us into a room with chrome-and-glass tables, with a large-screen projection TV showing American football."

"That's not on until later tonight. I hope we're home in time to see it. But I know what you mean."

"All we can do is wait and see."

We didn't have to wait long. The butler came back and said, "Tea is being served in the drawing room."

He led the us down the hallway, past several hundred square

yards of carved dark oak, into a room that looked like a set for one of the costume dramas on BBC1.

Lady Arking was in green today, a green as bright as the red she'd been wearing when I first met her. Apparently, she saved muted colors for incognito. She rose when we entered, and shook hands like a man.

The man in the room with her was a little slower on the uptake, but he also rose and shook. He was about half a head shorter than Lady Arking; he was built a little slight. He fit in quite well with the Christieland conceit, with sandy hair made two shades darker by whatever he used to slick it back, and the superior grin on his face. He left eye occasionally twitched, as though it were pining for a monocle.

"Hello, Cobb," he said. "Pleasure to meet you. Saw your exit from custody of the bobbies on telly. Brilliant, absolutely. Almost art. Worthy of a poem."

This was Stephen Arking, Lady Arking's stepson. His mother, Sir Richard's first wife, had died when Stephen was away at school.

Stephen was a poet. Or, as I was to hear for the first time in just a few seconds, he was "the" poet, though if he was ever published in anything he didn't have cash behind, I sure never heard of it.

He was dressed like *somebody's* idea of a poet, I suppose. Slacks, blazer, and the kind of tie Americans call an ascot. I expected a fish-grip handshake from him, but it was surprisingly firm and dry.

"It was all organized by Miss Schick," I said. "She's the brilliant one."

"Ah," Stephen said. "All the more pleasure, then, in doing this." He took Roxanne's hand and kissed it. "You and I have something in common, my dear. We must get together some day and talk about it."

"What's that?" Rox asked.

"We have both spurned communications empires that were

ours by birthright. Thank God I've had Pamela to run things. Lord knows I can't be bothered. How do you manage?"

Roxanne smiled sweetly. I knew that smile. Stephen was not making a really good first impression.

"I just mind my own business and cash the dividend checks," she said.

Stephen laughed. "Excellent," he said. "Absolutely excellent. Aren't they the most refreshing people we've met in ages, dear?"

That rang wrong. I didn't think even a blatant phony like Stephen Arking would look at his stepmother and think of calling her "dear."

Then I heard a quiet little voice say, "I think they're absolutely charming, darling."

I turned, looking for the owner of the voice. I found her after a few seconds, sitting on a chair in the corner. I literally had not noticed her until she spoke.

She was a tiny woman, maybe five feet tall and ninety pounds with her pockets full of change. She was dressed in a pink sweater and a long gray skirt. Once you noticed her, it was possible to see that she was quite pretty, in a china-doll sort of way, with a cap of strawberry-blond curls. Nice face, highlighted by bright blue eyes behind wire-frame spectacles.

This, I found out, was Phoebe Arking, Stephen's wife. I went over to her. She extended a hand as soft and fragile seeming as a six-year-old's. I kissed it. She actually blushed.

"Hey," I said, "fair is fair," and she smiled me a little bit of a smile.

Over sandwiches and cakes and tea, I learned a little bit about her. She wasn't much for talk, but she'd talk about Stephen. She had been working as a secretary in a literary agency and somehow came across some of Stephen's work and took the incredibly bold step of contacting him. Since then, apparently, her life had been bliss, married to Stephen Arking "the" poet.

It occurred to me that they might be happy together at that. He certainly looked as if he would enjoy having someone around to worship him.

I took a bite of a watercress sandwich, with the crust carefully trimmed off. My position on those things is this: British dairy products are so good, especially butter, that you can't ruin them even if you stick them between two wimpy pieces of bread with a piece of lawn clipping.

The maid (of course, there was a maid—who's gonna have a butler without any maids?) offered the tray of sandwiches to Phoebe, who studied it carefully, little pink lips pursed in thought. Finally, when I thought the maid was about to brain her with the silver tray, thereby tendering her resignation from Christieland on the spot, Phoebe came through and picked a cucumber sandwich.

With a bite daintily nibbled and gone, Phoebe made so bold as to speak again. "I saw it, too, you know. On television. The afternoon news. Your leaving . . ."

"Jail," I supplied.

"I don't know if it was art, as Stephen says. I'm not very clever about those things. But I think it was wonderfully brave."

"All I had to do was walk down a flight of steps."

"But the attention. The notoriety. I don't think I could bear it."

I shrugged. "In this case the notoriety was unavoidable. All Roxanne did was to try to shape it in my favor. I think she succeeded."

"Forgive me, Mr. Cobb, but why are you here? Pamela usually runs from scandal. Why does she have you to tea the very day something like this happens? Stephen doesn't show it, but he's very worried. What's going on?"

Lady Arking's imperious voice cut through like a guillotine blade. "That, Phoebe, is precisely what we are here to discuss."

# 10

*L*ady Arking went into executive mode.

The maids were told to leave the trays and the tea and depart. The butler was summoned.

"Banbridge," she said, "no calls. No interruptions of any kind."

Banbridge bowed his pink-and-purple head and said, "Very good, mum," and (not for the first time) I wanted to go up to him and pinch him and make sure he was real.

Stephen cleared his throat and adjusted his ascot. "I say, then, Pamela, Phoebe and I should be running along, too."

"No, Stephen, I wish you to stay. I know you have often said you have no interest in the running of your father's business, but the time may now have come when you wish to change your mind."

"Pamela, don't be daft. Father wanted you running the company, and so do I."

"My point," Lady Arking said, "is that after you hear what I have to say, you may not feel that way any longer."

She turned to me. "The first thing I want to do, Mr. Cobb, is apologize to you. I hope you can believe me when I say that when I asked you for what I thought was a simple favor, I had no idea it would turn out to be a nightmare for you."

"It wasn't the best night I ever spent," I said, "but nightmare is a little strong. Let's call it an inconvenience."

"You are very kind." She sipped tea. "More than kind. Sitting there in jail, you certainly had no reason to protect me, but you did."

"Just looking after my investment in the Network," I told her.

"You'll forgive me if I don't believe you. After what had happened, you had no reason to think protecting Pamela Arking was the same as protecting your investment."

Stephen's brow furrowed under the Byronic lock of hair that fell over it. "Pamela," he said, "do you mean to say you had something to do with that African's death?"

"Yes," she said, then thought about it a second. "No." Further reflection led her to an "I don't know."

The amazing thing about that was that all three answers were accurate.

"What she had to do with," I said, "was my being there."

I turned to her ladyship. "All right, I protected you—for the time being, pending this talk."

"Fair enough," she conceded.

"I knew there was some kind of mess-up, but I just didn't think you could be behind it."

"Why not?"

"Forgive me, Lady Arking, but this was—and is—a horribly haphazard business. If it was an intended frame, it would fall apart the second they tested my hands for firearms. Even as a straight rubout, it was pretty lame. Not only was the real killer seen, I came within a half second of catching him with the gun in his pocket. It just seemed to me that with your money and your connections, you could have bought a much better job."

"But I still don't understand," Stephen said. His brow hadn't smoothed out yet. His furrowing muscles must have been magnificently developed. "What did Pamela have to do with the fellow at all? And where do you come into it?"

"That," I said, "is the very question I've come here to ask."

Lady Arking took another sip of tea, put the cup down, and sighed. "There's no mystery about where you come into it, Mr. Cobb. I wanted someone reliable and discreet, who wouldn't immediately be associated with me. It was just as I told you when I asked you to meet Aliou in the first place."

"Well," I said, "I'm associated with you now. Bristow undoubtedly made the connection as soon as Williams walked into the police station."

"He did indeed. I was questioned yesterday afternoon and again, this morning."

This was news.

I waited until Stephen and Phoebe stopped gasping, and I said, "What did you say?"

"I told him any questions about me and my solicitors were highly improper, and that any questions about you and your solicitors should be asked of you."

I nodded. "Where it would also be highly improper. Did he ask how you knew me?"

"I told him only by way of a business relationship—what's the matter?"

She'd seen my frown.

"Well," I said, "don't take it back now, but don't play it up, either."

"Why not? We did meet in Bernard Levering's office, didn't we?"

"Yeah. But Roxanne and I are here on Independent Means visas. We can stay as long as we like, but we're not allowed to work. After this mess yesterday, the last thing I need is trouble with the Home Office for violating my visa."

"I'm so sorry," she said. "You see, Stephen, I've been making a right botch of things, and you haven't heard the worst of it yet."

She was harder on herself than she needed to be. I could see it was a natural mistake for her to have made. She was the kind of person who'd find it incomprehensible that anyone would deliberately set himself up not to work.

It was evident in the way she related to her stepson. She was being deferential to him now, because she'd put her foot in something (I *still* didn't know what), and he, having inherited a block of stock from Daddy, was in a position to cause trouble for her if he could work up the energy.

But she had no respect for him.

Even if Stephen Arking the poet slaved night and day and sweated blood to turn out his stuff, his stepmother didn't think of that as work. Even though he would have been a threat to her hegemony at BIC, something, word was, she protected only slightly more zealously than a wolverine protects her young, I got the feeling she would have liked Stephen a lot better if he had been out and about his father's business, poking his nose into things like newspapers and satellite TV networks.

It hadn't sunk into her yet that I was more or less retired, and for all she (or I) knew, was going to stay that way. Right now I was her fair-haired boy, but when she put it all together, my standing in the Christieland ratings would drop through the floor.

The idea was to work (in a non–visa-violating way, of course) fast.

"Tell me about Joseph Aliou," I said.

Again, she began with a sigh. It wasn't a fatalistic sigh, or a defeated one. It was more a sign of impatience with a world unwilling to run the way she had decided it ought to. "Joseph Aliou was a journalist." She tilted her head to one side, weighing it. "Yes," she said. "He had always wanted to be a journalist, and he died while working on a story. He was the finest kind of journalist."

Roxanne leaned over and whispered to me, "Yeah, he never hit her up for a raise." Despite her being a major owner of the Network, and therefore of Network News, Rox's personal experiences with the press have been less than rewarding. It's tended to warp her outlook.

"I first met him a few years ago. You see, he had worked as a stringer for Wolfrey Hawkesworth."

"Excuse me," I said, "who?"

"Wolfrey Hawkesworth," she said, the way she might have said, "Margaret Thatcher, you dunce." When I still didn't get it, she went on, "for many years the West African correspondent for the *Journal*."

I should have known. The *Journal* was BIC's other national newspaper in Britain, as respectable and staid as its sister paper, the *Orbit,* was wild and raunchy. It was hard to see how one person could own both without going completely schizo, but Pamela Arking managed it, as far as anyone could tell.

All the writers on the *Journal* have names like "Wolfrey Hawkesworth" and "Simon Purest" and "Cadwalader St. Buffington III." The name leads the jaded reader such as myself into the supposition the reporters who bear them are somehow classier than the ordinary run of journalists.

It might even be true.

Lady Arking went on to tell the tale of Joseph Aliou. He was a bright young man who'd grown up speaking French, pidgin, and a tribal language in Bafut, in Cameroon. A missionary school taught him English, by way of day-old copies of the *Journal* that came in the mail to satisfy the missionary's hunger to keep up with the news and cricket scores from England.

Joseph became entranced with the strange land described in the paper and decided he wanted to be a journalist himself. One day, the missionary took him to the capital (Joseph had never been there before) and introduced him to Wolfrey Hawkesworth, one of the legendary beings whose names appeared regularly on the good gray pages.

Joseph confessed his ambition in his ever-improving English, and the correspondent was so impressed, he gave the boy his business card and told him to contact him if he came across a good story.

Hawkesworth heard from him within a week, and it was a good story—tribal unrest; a plot to unseat the current Fon; possible bloodshed. It checked out, and Hawkesworth had a scoop.

Joseph Aliou proved particularly good at getting around and hearing things, and hardly a month went by without the boy tipping the reporter to a good, solid lead.

Hawkesworth paid the going rate for stringers. The missionary banked it for him. By the time he was twenty, Joseph had made himself a nice little pile, by hometown standards. But he had bigger ambitions. He wanted to go to university, in France, because as good as his English was, he didn't want to depend on getting his education in a language not his own. He would work on his English in his spare time.

"Which he did," Lady Arking said. "When I met him, two years ago, his English was only slightly accented. I was in Paris arranging for the European distribution of decoders for TVStrato, and taking the opportunity while I was there to meet with some of BIC's top foreign correspondents. Wolfrey had arranged a scholarship for Aliou; then, when he had his heart attack, he left Joseph enough money to finish his studies.

"Joseph had made a strong impression on me, as he did on virtually everyone he met. Wolfrey Hawkesworth had vouched for his journalistic instincts. I resolved to hire him as soon as his studies were done. But then, something came up. Something very unsettling."

"What was that?" I asked.

She shifted uneasily in her chair. It was the first time I'd seen anything from her that was less than queenly. Obviously, we were cutting close to the bone.

"Do you know anything about visa mills, Mr. Cobb?"

"A little," I said, as reality began to pull aside the curtain of Christieland. "There was a flurry about it in the papers when Roxanne and I first arrived."

I'd remembered what I'd learned.

As far as immigration to find a better life is concerned, America is still the Promised Land. But in the realities of the world economy at the end of the twentieth century, Mother England had become something of a Land of Opportunity herself, for people from countries with worse economies—i.e., virtually all of them, except the United States and Japan.

There are lots of ways to get permission to come and live in Britain. Some of them are so simple as to be nonexistent. If you're a citizen of another European Community country, you simply show up. A lot of them show up and sign up for public assistance. In my humble opinion, the United Kingdom has been played for a sucker in all the Common Market treaties it has ever been a party to, but as a mere visitor, I suppose that's none of my business, so I'll go on.

If you're a rich American, say, like Roxanne, or even me, you can get a long-term visa because of the dough you will be importing from home. This gives you most of the privileges of residence, but forbids you to work, on the theory that you might be taking a job away from a citizen. Fair enough.

Even if you're a relatively poor American, you can automatically get a visitor's visa for six months (twice what most other countries in Western Europe will give you), again, as long as you don't work.

If you want or need to go into the job market, though, things start getting a little tight. There are special provisions for people like writers (who create their own jobs, after all) and scientists.

But, as with all of life, the more you need permission to come to a free country and work to make a decent life for yourself, the harder it is to get.

So, while it's a snap for a successful American writer, say, to get permission to come to the United Kingdom and write and do whatever he likes, a poor African auto mechanic will go through hell for the same privilege.

There are, however, some loopholes.

One of the major loopholes is the student visa. Young William Jefferson Clinton, Rhodes scholar, had one of those years ago. A student visa carries with it National Health Insurance. It also carries a work permit.

The thing is, one does not need to be a Rhodes scholar to get one of them. One can go to the Hackney Wick School of Beauty Science and get one. One can, especially, go to the schools of English. You can find at least one, one flight up, in every high street in London.

Most of them are strictly legit. The Third Worlder (or Non-EC European) comes to England on a visitor's visa and enrolls in the school. The school then vouches for the enrollment, the pupil applies for a student visa, enabling him or her to work to pay for the classes, and proceeds to attend classes and learn the language.

A significant minority, though, are phonies. Visa mills. The so-called students pay the money, all right, but they never show up for classes. They couldn't if they wanted to, because the visa mill (a) probably doesn't have any actual teachers, just an office staff, and (b) they wouldn't have enough room to hold the classes, anyway, since they sign up many times more students than they could possible accommodate. They spend the rest of their time making fake visa certifications and counting money.

"So you brought Aliou over to do some undercover work in the visa-mill story?"

"That's right," Lady Arking said. "I figured he'd be perfect. He'd be totally unknown in Britain, he was keen to do the work and had a talent for it, and he was legitimately from a Third World country, with the passport to match."

"When did he start?"

"The beginning of September."

"Wasn't the story a little stale by then? In fact, I think the *Journal* and the *Orbit* had already run stories on it."

"I remember that myself," Stephen said.

Lady Arking showed us a wry smile.

"It may have been stale. It was freshened for me when I got this."

She walked to a an old ebony secretary, unlocked it, popped a secret drawer and took out a folded yellowish piece of cheap typing paper.

There was writing on it, or rather hand printing. Block capitals done in smeary ballpoint pen. It read:

> Hypocrite: You write about our only hope as "Visa Mills" and say you will put them out of business. You use the power of lies and false publicity. I know your dirty game. You're worse than all of them, and when all is known, you will be tarred by the same brush, you and your precious Sir Richard, the biggest visa racketeers of all.
>
> Remember

At a nod from Lady Arking, I passed it around. It made a big impression. Phoebe began trembling when she read it.

She looked up with tears in her eyes, from fear or anger, I couldn't tell which.

"This . . . this is horrid!" she announced to anybody hanging around who might be thinking otherwise. "Pamela, who sent this?"

"I don't know," Lady Arking said. "It's anonymous and, I'm afraid, untraceable. I had an independent laboratory examine it. The paper is ordinary Basildon bond, available at any newsagent in the country; the ink is generic Biro."

"What about the handwriting?" Stephen asked. He seemed concerned.

"The handwriting expert decided that the printing is the work of a right-handed person using his—or her, they couldn't even tell that much—left hand. And it's disguised as well. As I said, untraceable."

"Rats," I said. "I was hoping you were hanging on to a cream-colored monographed envelope."

Lady Arking smiled ruefully. "The envelope is more of the same, I'm afraid. I do have it. It was mailed in London."

"Wonderful," Roxanne said. "All you have to do is look for a right-handed person in London. There can't be more than nine million of them."

"Don't forget the commuters," I said.

"True," Rox replied.

"I took your point quite some time ago," Lady Arking said. "There was no point in pursuing the identity of the anonymous letter writer any further."

"But you took the suggestion of the letter seriously," I said.

"I had to. I am in a position of some responsibility as the Managing Director of BIC—"

"Caesar's wife was a slut by comparison," Stephen put in.

"That will be enough, Stephen." Lady Arking turned to me. "The joke was tasteless, Mr. Cobb, but accurate. How am I to crusade against victimizations of the visa-mill variety if I am liable to a charge of corruption myself?"

She spoke with real passion. Then she caught herself at it and harrumphed it off.

"When I say 'myself' in this context, I mean me, or any of my staff, or anyone connected with British International Communications. Malfeasance on anyone's part can destroy our effectiveness."

"Did you, or do you, have any reason to suspect the charge might be true?"

"No," she said flatly. "No specific reason. But, don't you see, it was something I had to know."

"Is the corporation, or you, or was your husband, maybe, involved in a school or schools—even legitimate ones—in any way?"

"What are you insinuating, Mr. Cobb?"

"Relax, I'm not insinuating anything. I'm trying to find out what was going on in the sender's mind."

"Mischief," the lady insisted. "Troublemaking, pure and simple."

"No, ma'am," I said. "Not so pure and not so simple at all. You sent Joseph Aliou out to sign up at a bunch of English schools, didn't you?"

"Yes," she said. "Yes, I did. We had a list of schools that we suspected, but couldn't prove, were bogus."

"And I assume the idea was for him to let drop some sort of tentative connection with BIC, maybe a grudge he had against them or something?"

Lady Arking nodded half-admiringly. "You've done this sort of investigation before, then, Mr. Cobb."

"Yes, I have, God help me. Look, Aliou was looking into this, and he got shot to death. Whatever's going on here, it's a lot dirtier and more dangerous than mere mischief."

"Yes, of course. I'll answer your question. No, to my knowledge, neither I, nor the corporation, nor Richard in a private capacity had or has any connection with a school of any kind."

"What about members of the staff?"

"I wouldn't know about that. It's in their contracts that they may not invest in any rival communications companies, but we take no notice of how they invest their private funds otherwise."

I frowned. It was the decent way to run a business, of course, but it made for some damned inconvenient investigating.

"Stephen," I said.

He jumped. "What?" Then he grinned self-consciously. "You quite startled me, you know."

"Sorry. Do you live by the fruits of poetry alone, or do you have any investment in a school or a chain of schools or something else like that?"

"No, poetry these days is a forest bereft of fruit. If I depended on it for my living, I should be deceased by now. Fortunately, BIC has never failed to declare a dividend, and that manna is gathered and husbanded by Phoebe, the well-named light of my life. We don't want for anything, do we, dear?" he asked.

"No, Stephen," she said. "Mr. Cobb, why are you doing this? Pamela was the victim of the anonymous letter. *We* surely don't know anything about it. You sound so—so *accusatory*."

I shook my head. "That's not what I'm driving at. You've read the letter. It's grammatical and spelled correctly—unusual in anonymous letters, by the way; we get thousands of them at the Network—but it's hardly a model of clarity, is it? I mean the person who wrote this was either in the midst of severe nervous agitation, or giving a good impression of feeling that way.

"Can it be a pack of lies? Sure it can, but if it is, they're lies covering up something equally sinister—the death of Aliou shows that.

"But I'm pursuing something else. What if the person who wrote the letter is sincere but mistaken? If they've noticed something significant and misinterpreted it?"

There was a chorus of "ahs" as the message got through.

"You see? If you can figure out what someone might have gotten wrong, you *might* be able to figure out who it is. Then we could learn what else he knows."

"Or she," Roxanne said.

"Or she. Don't just shake your heads. Keep it in mind and think about it for a while."

"Excellent, Mr. Cobb. I might never have thought of this."

"BIC needs a department of Special Projects."

"Fine idea," she said. "Start one for me. Handle this business.

Establish the department in full when it's taken care of. Name your own price."

Out of the corner of my eye I could see Roxanne's luscious lips tighten, and saw her draw her shoe back to kick me in the ankle if I gave the slightest sign I was going to acquiesce.

"Ha!" I said rudely. Rox's leg relaxed. "With all due respect, Lady Arking, ha! And also, ha-ha! It was exactly this kind of work that drove me out of New York, my hometown, and away from the Network in the first place. I suggest you get a good private eye to look into the murder of Joseph Aliou. If you want recommendations of names for special-project head, I can help you there, too. But as far as personal involvement with this matter goes, as far as I'm concerned, it ends with whatever advice I can give you this afternoon."

She didn't like it, that much was evident in the frozen look that came over her face. She was, however, too well bred to give the typical American reaction (you can't walk out on me now, you bastard). Or maybe she was living up to her house.

She took about half a minute to get it swallowed, then said, "I see. Is there no way I can persuade you to continue with this? You've been so helpful already."

"No, ma'am. You couldn't pay me to do it; even if I needed the money, if I took it, I would violate the terms of my visa. I really need to get away from this sort of thing. I attract murder the way other people attract the opposite sex. I did a simple favor for you, and look what happened."

"Of course. I shall pay your solicitor."

I was mad at myself. I was over here trying to save what was left of my sanity and my humanity. I didn't owe Lady Arking a thing; in fact, I had already delivered more for her than any reasonable person could expect. Yet I sat there in that drawing room feeling like a total shit who had let the side down badly.

"Thank you," I said. "There's just one thing I wanted to know about."

Stephen left no doubt of what he thought of me. "Why bother, old man, if you're no longer involved?"

God, I thought, when a *poet* holds you in contempt, you are really belly down to the bottom.

"Because," I said, "I've got the kind of brain that won't be bossed. If I have enough facts, I might think of something helpful, even if I'm not involved."

Lady Arking sounded weary. "Ask your question, Mr. Cobb."

"What was the five thousand pounds about?"

"Aliou had told me he needed some money to pay for information. And to live on. He had to live like an immigrant on the make, as you Americans would say, but it wasn't necessary for him to starve."

"So he was going to schmear somebody," I mused. "I wonder who."

I stood up. Rox followed suit.

"Well," I said, "if you follow my advice, and hire a good PI to look into this for you, the place to have him start is the W. G. Peterson School of English."

"I believe that was on the list."

"Well, when Aliou switched envelopes with me, the one he gave me for you had a brochure from there in it."

"A what?" Stephen demanded.

"A broacher."

"Oh."

I was about to make our awkward replies when a flustered Banbridge burst most unbutlerlike into the room.

"Beg pardon, mum, but the gentlemen—I couldn't prevent—the police."

And it was the police, right behind him.

Specifically, it was Detective Inspector Bristow. When he saw me, his face lit up with a good imitation of delight.

"Jackpot!" he said. "Imagine, Griffiths," he said to the black detective accompanying him, "*everyone* we wanted to talk to in one place."

He made a slight bow. "Lady Arking, I'm afraid we shall have to talk to you again. And to Mr. and Mrs. Stephen Arking. We missed them last night. I should like to do it myself, but instead, I am going to leave you in the capable hands of DC Griffiths, who has been to university.

"Mr. Cobb, however, is going to come with me."

# 11

Not again!" Roxanne screamed.

She looked as if she were about to kick him in the ankle.

"Quiet, Rox," I said. "What happened, Bristow? Lose the gun-shot test?"

"No, no," he said. "Everything's fine on that score. Just something I'd like to consult you about. You seem to be doing that fairly freely, and I thought I'd avail myself, in the interest of transatlantic relations, as it were."

"Lady Arking," I said distinctly, "asked us for tea."

"Of course she did, and what a good idea, too. You're the most charming of guests, as I learned last night. So full of ideas and conversation, isn't he, Lady Arking?"

I spoke to her before she could answer. "There's no sense in making a scene about it," I said. "I'll go along with the inspector—"

"Me, too," Rox added grimly.

"A call to Williams might be in order," I said. "Just in case."

"I shall be calling my solicitor straightaway, in any case, Mr. Cobb. Williams will be standing by for you."

"Very good," I said. "If Miss Schick can't come along, she will follow, find out where I am, and call for Williams as soon as I need him."

"I really don't think you'll need him tonight," Bristow said mildly. "I simply need your assistance with some of our enquiries."

"As Inspector Dew undoubtedly said to Crippen."

"My goodness, Mr. Cobb, the people you will compare yourself to. And poor Miss Schick. Excuse me for being personal, Miss, but having seen your performance on the steps of the nick this morning, I doubt that you could ever masquerade as a boy."

"I've never even been tempted." To me, she said, "Matt, what is this asshole talking about?"

"Way to turn on the old charm, honey." I turned to Bristow. "All right," I said, "I'm ready to come along." I stuck out my wrists, but Bristow just looked at me reproachfully.

"We'll dispense with that this evening," he said, leaving me to wonder whether he meant the handcuffs, the badinage, or both.

I decided it was both, and gave him a break in the two minutes it took to get our coats and be escorted down to the sidewalk.

Then I said, "Where are we going? You'll noticed I waited until we were outside before I asked that."

"Yeah," he said, "You're Mr. Consideration himself, you are. We're going, if you absolutely insist on knowing, to the morgue. The Battersea Morgue, to be precise."

"It's always nice to be precise," I said.

"Am I coming or not?" Roxanne demanded.

Bristow thought it over for a minute.

"Might as well, darlin'," he said at last. "I saw your performance this morning. If I don't bring you along, you're likely to show up in a circus wagon and all."

Roxanne's smile gleamed in the street lights. "You never know."

"All right, come on then."

We climbed into the back of a really nice car, a big Jaguar, with a driver yet.

"Not bad," I said. "Who pays the driver, the department or you?"

Bristow took out a cigar, bit the end off, lowered a window electronically, and spat.

"You know, Cobb," he said, "just when I get to thinking you might not be such a bad sort after all, you go and get up my nose all over again."

"My heart bleeds," I said. "Listen, you could stand me up your nose like this for two and a half years and still not be even for the stunt you pulled on me last night, and you know it."

"I was trying to keep the peace," he said.

"Yeah, Gandhi Bristow, they call him around the nick. You're not planning to light that thing, are you?"

"I'm allergic," Roxanne lied.

Bristow said, "Grrr," and put it back in his pocket. The driver, a big, red-haired Irish-looking guy, snickered. It was the only sound I ever heard him make. Bristow gave him a dirty look.

"So," I said jauntily, "who's dead?"

"You're jumping to conclusions, Cobb."

I shook my head, realized that Bristow, in the front seat, couldn't see it, then said, "No, I'm reaching logical conclusions. If I were back under arrest or in danger of being, you would have slapped me down before I'd even ruffled the first nostril hair."

"Don't be disgusting."

"It's your metaphor, not mine. Anyway, a man on his way back to the clink would have had more respect forced on him. And I didn't figure you'd be hauling me off to the morgue because you like to see the Battersea Power Station by moonlight. Therefore, somebody's dead—either to do with this case or another one, and you've got to be there. The question is, do I?"

• • •

And that remained the question, right up through the time we entered the place.

It occurred to me that practically every morgue I've ever been in (granted, it's been fewer than five, but I bet that's more than you've been in. I hope so, at least, for your sake—it isn't the kind of excursion you take for fun) has been near a river.

Knowing what lay ahead, I asked Roxanne if she wanted to wait in the anteroom, but it's a funny thing about morgues. Any living person hanging around, even somebody you'd trust your baby to in an emergency in any other place, instantly becomes suspect.

Rox, deciding she'd feel safer among the dead, said she'd stick with me.

It was downstairs to the accommodations. The unmistakable smell greeted us, the gallons of antiseptic, and the dark, fetid, slightly sweet smell the antiseptic never quite manages to get rid of.

Bristow pulled the cigar out of his pocket again, and looked at it wistfully. "Pity Miss Schick is allergic," he said.

I looked at Roxanne, who was slightly green but determined. "Oh, what the heck," she said. Her voice sounded slightly strangled, which was, I guess, appropriate. "Go ahead."

"You're sure, now?" he said.

She grabbed him by the wrist. "Light the goddamn thing," she said. "Just light it, okay?"

"With pleasure." Bristow smiled.

He did, too, puffing and sucking on the thing until the end glowed cherry red behind a coating of gray. It certainly was nicer to smell the place wrapped in a cocoon of smoke than it was otherwise. Bristow had obviously been in more morgues than I had.

Your brain is your worst enemy in a place like that. Most morgues are clean and well lit and labored in by healthy and well-educated individuals dressed in immaculate white outfits. Your imagination, however, insists on hearing water dripping, and rats scuttling in nonexistent dark corners, and expects to see a hairy hunchback behind every rank of drawers.

The morgue attendant who waved hello to DI Bristow and showed us the way to locker number 2467Z (pronounced "zed") was a tall young fellow with a blond crew cut who could have been a guard on a U.S. high school basketball team circa 1958. The only visible thing wrong with him was acne.

The kid stifled a yawn and grabbed the handle of the cabinet.

"Wait!" I said.

"What's wrong now?" Bristow demanded.

What was wrong was that Roxanne's shoulder had bumped mine about three times in the last minute. It could mean nothing, or it could mean she was getting a little rocky on her pins.

She appeared a little woozy when I looked at her. I said, "Rox, before he opens the drawer, I want you to be aware of something."

"What's that?"

"The first time I was inside one of these places, and they pulled the drawer open, I went blind and deaf for thirty seconds. If you want to be honest about it, you can say I more or less fainted on my feet."

"Lost my lunch, I did," Bristow said mildly. He kept puffing his cigar. He reminded me of The Little Engine That Could.

"It's a natural reaction. There's survival value in being upset by the presence of death. It may not be especially smart to train ourselves out of it, but we do. So whatever happens, it's nothing to be ashamed of, okay?"

She managed a little smile and nodded. "Okay," she said.

This time, the kid with the acne didn't bother to stifle the yawn. He thumbed the latch, pulled the handle, and slid out the drawer.

It was loud—ridiculously, incredibly loud. They must do something to the damn things to make that particular rolling, grinding noise reverberate so thoroughly through your soul.

Roxanne did fine. She gripped my arm near the elbow and squeezed tight, but she didn't faint, and she didn't bring up any of Lady Arking's watercress sandwiches, either.

It helped that the stiff in question was not gruesome, as these things go. It wasn't visibly decayed or dismembered or anything like that. The eyes were open, but that was just gravity. Without muscles to hold them closed, eyelids usually fall open. The effect in this case was to give the face an expression of surprise and distaste, as though he'd just found a caterpillar in his salad.

There were three brownish holes in the torso, but the body had been washed, and from a distance (which I hoped Rox would keep) they didn't look a whole lot worse than, say, hickeys.

"Recognize him?" Bristow asked.

"Sure do," I said.

"You do?" Rox demanded. Puzzlement brought a little color back to her cheeks.

"Who is it?" Bristow said. "For the record."

"Well, I don't know his name," I said. "But it's who I expected it to be. It's the guy in the crowd outside Planet Hollywood on Sunday. The one who shot Joseph Aliou."

"Don't be hasty now," Bristow cautioned. "Take your time."

There was no sense arguing with him; he even had a point. So I looked again. The complexion was a little paler, but what the hell, the guy was dead. I'd had a good look and the features were the same. This was the man who'd shot Joseph Aliou. I was sure of it. I told Bristow as much.

"Sure of that, are you?"

"Jesus Christ, Bristow, talk about getting up somebody's nose. You get up mine and into all eight sinus cavities. How many times do I have to answer a question? It's him. Have somebody write it down and I'll sign it."

Bristow looked tired, frustrated, and depressed. "We'll do that later. Right now, how about the two of you coming to lift a couple of pints with me?"

I was inclined to look a gift horse in the mouth, but Roxanne raised her eyes to heaven and said, "Great, let's get out of here."

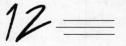

**"He's terrific, he's magnific,**

**"He's the strongest, he's the bravest, he's the best!"**

Theme song
*Danger Mouse,* Thames TV

*B*ristow brought us to a place not far from the morgue. I expected it to be called the Formaldehyde and Scalpel or something like that, but it turned out to be the Green Man, like at least five hundred eighty-seven other pubs in London, to say nothing of the rest of England.

I suppose, though, if a significant proportion of the clientele staggered in there for fortification after a session at the morgue, the name could have a certain appropriateness for this particular establishment that the others lacked.

At that, this was an okay place. A lot of pubs have been Americanized, offering English approximations of pizza and nachos, with jukeboxes blaring. This place, though, retained the kind of Englishness that Americans come to England to see in the first place and fail to find, because so much of British culture is a mad scramble to catch up with U.S. culture of three years ago.

Mostly, when a tourist finds something that seems English

through and through, it's something that's been carefully calculated to be that way expressly to catch the tourist trade.

But tourists don't go to Battersea (and most of them don't go to Barnes, come to that), and the Green Man was simply what it was—an English pub with an established clientele, one that didn't have to struggle to be hip.

So there was no jukebox, just a small TV over the bar showing soccer highlights. No pizza, just a platter of Scotch eggs down one end of the bar.

A Scotch egg is a hard-boiled egg that is shelled, coated in sausage meat, dipped in the toxic orange breadcrumbs they use in England, and then fried. They really are remarkable-looking constructions. Bristow grabbed one as we walked in, yelled, "Hey, Tel" to the barman and showed it to him, then led us to a table in the back.

"Missed my dinner," he said, and took half the thing in one bite.

"Jesus," Roxanne breathed and turned her head away.

Bristow seemed genuinely sorry. "Oh, goodness, miss, I didn't realize." He stuffed the rest of the thing in his mouth.

"All right," he said, still chewing. "All gone now."

Just about the time Rox decided it was safe to look again, a handsome, hennaed, middle-aged woman proudly wearing a low-cut blouse came to the table. She kissed Bristow on his bald spot, greeted us with a big smile, and asked for orders.

Bristow asked for a pint of Youngs, and I went along with him.

"How about you, love?" she asked Rox.

"Lemonade, please," Rox ordered. In Europe, "lemonade" means an extremely sweet carbonated beverage.

"Actually, Miss," Bristow said, being helpful, "after your visit, you might want something a bit stronger."

Roxanne doesn't drink. She's convinced that having been hooked on drugs once, she's a walking invitation to another addiction. She may even be right. She can get pretty testy when people urge her to do something she doesn't want to, but she said, "Lemonade will be fine," and Bristow and the barmaid left her alone.

The pleasant clatter and chatter of a bunch of guys playing skittles in the open area of the pub came to us, and I took a deep breath. This was turning out okay on a night that had started out with my thinking I was going to be arrested again. Instead, I'd gone from Christieland to Edgar Wallaceland with only a brief stop at reality in between.

Soon our drinks came. Roxanne sipped her lemonade (it's the only way you can drink the stuff) and Bristow and I took long pulls at our nutty brown ale.

Then Bristow put his glass down on the table, sighed mightily, and muttered, "Oh, bloody 'ell."

I tried in vain to stifle a laugh. That was the other kind of show you were likely to tune in on when you switched on British TV at random—a bunch of people sitting around a pub, looking into their ale and saying, "Bloody 'ell, bloody 'ell."

"This is funny to you, is it?"

"Not really," I said. "No disrespect meant. It was just something I thought of. It would take too long to explain."

"I believe you, Cobb," he said. "When I first met you I had a premonition that nothing about you would be easy to explain. Come on, drink up. You should be celebrating."

"I'm completely off the hook, I take it."

"Completely. A bobby found our friend huddled in a doorway of an abandoned shop not far from the London Bridge tube station. Nudged him to move him along, saw the bullet holes when he fell over. He'd been killed somewhere else and brought, you see."

"Who was it?"

"Turned out to be a hood named Winston Blake. Twenty-four years old, plenty of form. Colleague of mine in Brixton who knew

*Killed in the Fog*  **107**

him said he'd always known our Winston would wind up on one end of a murder or the other. Turned out to be both."

"Solid?"

"Solid as can be. He was found with murder weapon on him, stuck in his back pocket. And the nitric-acid test showed that he had fired a gun recently."

I saw loopholes.

"I may be silly for pointing this out, but that's not airtight. It doesn't prove he fired the murder weapon at Aliou—just that he fired *something*. The murder weapon might have been planted on him later."

Bristow took a long swallow of bitter. It was the first time I'd ever seen him enjoy anything. "Might have been," he conceded, "but I know bloody well that *you* didn't do it, don't I? About the time Winston was getting his American sporting kit ventilated, *you* were in the nick, telling me what a right ruddy bastard I am. And Miss Schick was at home, having gone straight there after showing up on Lady Arking's doorstep."

"You had her followed? I didn't even know you knew about her until this morning."

"Ah, but that's because you didn't know she stood on the pavement after the wagon had taken you off for five minutes screaming curses at my men like a whole village full of fishwives."

Roxanne sipped her lemonade and looked very demure. "I was upset," she said.

"So I *am* off the hook," I said. Not that I had been on too securely at any point, but there is a difference between running around loose because the cops don't think they have enough evidence, and being loose because they do have enough evidence, and the evidence says you didn't do it.

"Right," Bristow said. "So celebrate."

I lifted my glass and drank. It was damn good beer.

"You said Winston got his American sports kit ventilated. Literally? He was still wearing it when he was found?"

"Exactly as you described him," Bristow said. Then he frowned. "You're an American. Why do you think that bloody stuff is so popular here? It's not like the sports themselves are, just the kit of the American teams."

"Integrity," I said.

"Integrity? What's that supposed to mean?"

"I mean that if you want a souvenir of the Orlando Magic, God knows why, it has 'Magic' written on it. If you buy something representing the Kansas City Chiefs, you get an arrowhead symbol. If you try to buy a Chelsea football jersey, it's got the name of some goddamn Dutch beer plastered across it, or some Japanese TV, I forget which. It's bad enough for the players to be renting out their chests as billboards. For a fan, I think it would be downright embarrassing."

"Well, it's a thought. I never thought I'd find an American TV executive denouncing commercialism."

"I'm not denouncing commercialism. I love commercialism. I'm saying get it right. A sports team is basically selling its fans identity and permanence. It's more like a religion than anything else. The identity of the team has to be paramount. Instead of companies paying the teams to advertise the product, in the States the teams charge companies for the privilege of identifying themselves with it. The New York Yankees don't have CANON plastered across their chests, but Canon does promote itself as 'the official camera of the New York Yankees.' See the difference?"

Bristow was sitting there with his mouth slightly open. I was afraid I'd lost him.

"So you're a philosopher, too, then," he said. "Miss Schick, I think you ought to know you've linked yourself up with a truly amazing man."

Roxanne twinkled. "He's got possibilities," she said.

"More than possibilities. I've spent a lot of time with the phone

*Killed in the Fog* **109**

to my earhole over the last twenty-four hours, most of it to New York, and I wouldn't mind facing St. Peter with the sort of recommendations he's gotten."

He put his hand on his heart. "Honestly, Miss. To hear the New York Police Department tell it, he's a cross between Sherlock Holmes, Abraham Lincoln, and John Wayne, he has that much brains, virtue, and courage. Good to his mum, too, his secretary tells me."

This was getting embarrassing.

"Ex-secretary," I said.

Bristow ignored me. "Matthew Cobb," he pronounced, "is apparently such a paragon, that I was right embarrassed in the knowledge that I had had him in the nick."

He finished his pint (twenty ounces to a pint in England) and waved for another.

"He is, I can only conclude," Bristow said, getting louder and louder as he went, "the absolute pinnacle of modern Anglo-American manhood—"

"He's pretty good in bed, too," Rox said.

I nearly sprayed bitter all over the bar. "Roxanne!" I said.

She was laughing her head off.

"Did it, by God," she was crowing. "Did it at last! All these years, and I've finally seen Cobb blush! You're blushing, Cobb."

"Lovely shade, too," Bristow added admiringly. "Sort of a bridal-suite pink, wouldn't you say?"

"I don't know," Rox said demurely. "I've never been inside a bridal suite."

"For God's sake," I said, "let's not get started on that again."

At that, I was almost treated to a sight I suspected was every bit as rare as me blushing—Bristow laughing. The corners of his mouth definitely twitched a few times, but he managed to control himself.

"Quite right, quite right," he said. "Can't be going off on tangents, now, can we? Not when we've still a long list of the man's virtues to catalog."

"Don't start *that* again, either," I said.

"Oh well, if you insist. I was quite warming to the task, though."

"Just cool off."

"I will in just a moment, if you please, after I have made my original point."

"There was a point? I mean, other than extracting as much Michael from me as possible?"

"Yes, there was a point. As before, I shall address my remarks to Miss Schick, who has a proper appreciation of them."

I don't think it was the beers that were making Bristow so . . . so whatever he was. He'd only had one and a couple of swallows of the other. I had to accept he was just being playful, something I previously would have rated somewhere below Jane Fonda's elevation to the papacy on a scale of likelihood. I wondered how many other undiscovered sides he was still hiding.

Bristow turned to Roxanne and said, "My point, my dear, is this: In the face of all the undeniable evidence of Cobb's preeminence as a human being, a solver of crimes, and as other things too delicate for a stranger such as myself to mention, why is he so sodding awful to me?"

"What do you mean?" Rox asked.

"I'm off to the loo," I said.

Roxanne took me by the hand. "Stick around," she ordered. "This won't be nearly so much fun if you're not around to be embarrassed by it."

"Here, we have a perfect little scenario. Little Winston, a noted thug, finally makes the big time, and does his first contract murder. But he picks his employer unwisely, and gets three bullets in the ticker instead of a roll of the liquid readies."

"That's how I read it," I said. Bristow looked at me. "For what it's worth," I added.

"What's wrong with that?" Rox asked.

Her he deigned to answer. "What is wrong with it is that it leaves one little question unanswered. I mean, we would still have an investigation on our hands, but it would be one set in the nice, wholesome squalor of the underworld. You and your class of friends would be completely out of it, and good riddance. If we had the answer to one little question."

Roxanne asked him what the question was, but I already knew.

Bristow told her. "What was he doing with those sodding money orders?"

"I'd hoped you'd have forgotten about those," I said.

"Oh, right, fat chance of that with the chief inspector on my arse every fifteen minutes about this case. Believe me, Jack Bristow isn't likely to forget anything associated with this case."

"Wait here," I said.

"What? Oh, off to the loo, eh?"

"I'm going," I said, "to make a phone call."

I went to the loo first. I found more evidence for my conclusion that England has been declared the international testing ground for finding out how many different ways you flush a toilet. This particular one had a chrome knob in the middle of the tank lid, which you had to pull up, then plunge down, as if you were setting off a charge of dynamite. Made about the same amount of noise, too.

After that, I found a phone along the wall not far from the bathroom. There are almost as many kinds of pay phones in England as there are kinds of toilets, some of which do not accept coins but only deduct money from a prepurchased magnetic card.

This was the kind wherein if you didn't push the little red button marked "A" after the other party answered the phone, your voice could not be heard and your money was wasted. I have spent the better part of several rainy mornings trying to figure out what purpose this procedure serves, but aside from being a way to make sure nobody too dumb to figure out the red button (me, for instance, the first three times) gets to make a phone call, I haven't made a lot of progress on it.

The phone rang, three chirps, then two at a time. It took a while. I pictured Banbridge toddling along on old, sore legs to pick up the phone.

It was a true picture.

"Arking House," Banbridge announced.

"Hello, Banbridge, this is—"

"Hello? Hello? Are you there?"

God *damn* it, I thought vehemently, and jabbed the stupid red button so hard I hurt my finger.

"Hello, Banbridge," I tried again. "This is Matt Cobb. I'd like to talk to Lady Arking, please."

"I'm not sure that will be possible, sir," he said.

"Why not?" I demanded. I was pretty indignant about it, too. Here I was going out of my way to phone the woman when I really had no duty or obligation to, and a butler was giving me this crap.

Then I caught myself, and I decided I had been listening to Bristow a little too eagerly when he'd been laying it on so thick about how great I was.

My tone had been sharpish, but Banbridge was unruffled. "She may not be able to come to the phone, sir."

"Will you find out, please?"

"I shall do so straightaway, sir."

"Straightaway" used up the rest of my original twenty pence, and I fed more coins into the phone, hoping I had enough.

The little liquid crystal display near the red button informed me that I had used up another thirty pence listening to silence, when a voice came on the line.

"Mr. Cobb?"

"Ah, Lady Arking." At last, I thought.

"The police are still here," she informed me.

*Killed in the Fog* **113**

"Oh," I said, "are they being impertinent?"

"I don't think I could say that, in fairness," she admitted reluctantly. "But they are being remarkably thorough to no purpose that is visible to me."

Up until then, I hadn't been completely sure how I felt about Pamela Arking, but at that moment, I decided that I loved her. I've known a lot of rich people in my time, and powerful ones, and for the vast majority of them, the question of fairness never has a damn thing to do with whether they think you're impertinent.

"It's okay," I said. "They're still here, too."

"Oh. Is it horrid?"

"No, actually, we're at a pub, and Bristow thinks he's standing us drinks. I'm not going to let him, of course."

"Have you had another idea?"

"Sort of," I said. "I've changed my mind. I'll handle the case for you."

"Oh," she said, sounding more like a schoolgirl than I would have believed possible. "That's wonderful. Come to the office tomorrow, and we'll make all the arrangements."

"Hold on a second. You may not think it's so wonderful when I tell you what I have in mind."

"Go ahead."

"We won't make any arrangements, and I'm not coming into your office. This is going to be tricky enough to handle without my running around inviting the Home Office to throw me out of the country."

"I've told you, that can be arranged."

"I don't want it arranged. I like it fine the way it is."

"All right," she said, and I loved her even more. No arguments, no "Now see here, young man." It was great.

"Now," I said, "here's the part you won't like: The cops have to know about Aliou."

"Oh. May I ask why?"

"Sure, you may ask why. The answer is that the killer will never be caught if we don't tell them."

"I see. Then there's no choice then, is there?"

With that, her conquest of my heart was complete. There are plenty of people with higher priorities than catching the murderer of a relative stranger.

I told her I'd fill in Bristow, but she might as well make a few Brownie points by turning loose of it herself to the cops there. Then I explained what Brownie points were, hung up the phone, and went back to the bar to get back up Bristow's nose.

## 13

### "Don't mention the War!"

John Cleese
*Fawlty Towers*, BBC

*R*oxanne was wearing her historian suit Wednesday morning, a simple blue jacket and skirt thing over a white silk blouse, a gold pin, a string of pearls, with her dark hair tied back at the nape of her neck with a white scarf.

She was also wearing a pair of gold-wire-frame glasses.

"Why do you wear those things?" I said.

"Why does anybody wear glasses?" she replied.

"Usually, to correct their vision. That's why I know you're a fraud. You don't wear contacts, and I happen to know you can read the fine print on a packet of artificial sweetener at fifty paces. The glasses are pure disguise. I'm just curious about why you wear them."

She made a face. "It's embarrassing," she said. "I'll sound conceited."

"You," I told her, "have a lot to be conceited about," I said.

"That's why I keep you around," she told me. "I love to hear you talk."

She slid the glasses down her nose and looked at me over the top of them. She was gathering things up ready to go; I was at the breakfast table with the international edition of *USA Today,* finishing the last of my French toast and soaking up all the football and basketball news I could find. The one thing I really missed here was TV coverage of Giants and Knicks games. If Rox and I were going to settle down here for a long time, I might invest in a really serious satellite dish, one that would pull in programs from the States as well as TVStrato.

"So what's the conceited reason?" I asked.

"I'm dressing down," she said. "I'm pretty young for the circles I've been moving in lately, and most of the time I still dress like a kid. And since I border on the attractive—"

"False modesty doesn't become you, honey. You're a knockout."

"I have short legs, my ears stick out, and my lips are too full."

It occurred to me that I've never known a woman who wasn't ready with an instant catalog of her shortcomings in the looks department, real or imagined.

"But," Rox went on, "I do admit that in these circles I am fairly glamorous, if only by default."

"So?"

"So I don't *want* to be. I've worked like crazy in the field to get people to ignore the fact that I've got money. I don't intend to have them dismiss me as a scholar because I happen to be good-looking. So I do whatever I can to downplay that."

I stuck out my lower lip. "Too bad," I said.

"I know," she said. "In a better world we'd be judged only on the quality of our work, but for now we all bring a lot of baggage with us whatever we do."

"No," I said. "Too bad because your plan doesn't work."

"What do you mean?"

"I mean that right this second you are the most delicious-looking thing on earth, and if we didn't have important things to do, I would be peeling that suit right back off you."

She smiled at me. "That's why God made the nighttime," she said.

Then she asked me what I was smiling at.

"I was reflecting on the fact that we're so far north it gets dark about a quarter after four in the afternoon in London this time of year."

"Just make sure you wait for me," she said.

"I'm hardly going to start without you."

"Just don't start with anyone else."

"What's that supposed to mean?"

"You're going to lunch with Phoebe Arking today."

"Yeah. I want to find out what the cops were asking them the other night. We're building a fine relationship with Bristow, but we haven't gotten to the point yet where he'll just let me walk in and read the police reports."

" 'Yet,' " she said. "I don't like this word, 'yet.' "

"I didn't mean I was going to keep working on him until he would. For God's sake, I didn't want to get involved in this. I'm only doing it because I want to get it over sooner."

"Famous last words," she said, then raised a hand. "I'm not calling you a liar, Cobb. I'm just lamenting Fate."

Now she waved the hand around, erasing the last few sentences. "But this is off the point, anyway," said. "I was talking about little Phoebe. Watch out for her."

"Huh?"

"I saw the way she was looking at you the other night. She wants your bod."

"Oh, come on, Rox. She's totally besotted with Stephen Arking, the Poet."

"And you were afraid of getting cynical," she said. "Sometimes you're so innocent, I hardly know you, Cobb. Phoebe is besotted with being married to *a* poet. With money. And having a stepmother-in-law named Lady. As if that proved anything. I had a dog named Lady once."

"And so she's going to make a move on me?"

"It's possible. You're dashing. You're glamorous, solving murders and all. In a weird sort of way, you're even handsome. She's a reach-for-the-stars type, the way I used to be, only she didn't do what I did to get cured of it."

"What's that?"

"Reached for the stars and wound up having to be rescued from a shit pile. She idealized her poet; she can idealize you the same way. She went after the poet, and she got him, but now she's used to the poet."

"And you worried about being conceited," I said. "Your humility is staggering. Phoebe Arking—*ten* Phoebe Arkings could never get me. I am already got."

She bent over and kissed me on the forehead. "Don't you forget it," she said.

"I am good and got," I told her. "Sheesh, the things you worry about."

"I wasn't actually worried," she said. "I just think when women look as if they're going to throw themselves at you, you should at least *notice*. Then I can feel triumphant, that you picked me over competition, instead of just keeping me on through inertia."

"You have no competition," I told her.

"I love you, Cobb."

I told her ditto, and she left. After a quick call to Bernard to brief him (something I'd promised Lady Arking to do last night), so did I.

I picked up Phoebe at the modest row house she shared with the Poet in Kensington. Modest, that is, by Schick and Arking standards. The average Londoner, or New Yorker even, would find it pretty ritzy. Phoebe was wearing a green sweater today, and the skirt was a different floral pattern, but the look was exactly the same as it had been Monday at tea; sort of a post-hippie waif look, like a flower child hurt and bewildered by an early frost.

She was chirpy today.

"I'm so pleased to get a chance to get to know you better, Matt—may I call you Matt?"

"Sure, all my friends do."

"And you must call me Phoebe. I know it's a horrid name, but I'm used to it."

"It means 'light bringer,'" I said.

"Yes, I knew that. Are you a student of the classics, Matt?"

"Not Latin and Greek ones, no. I just pick up a lot of little facts."

"Stephen took a first in Classics at Oxford, but he never uses classical allusions in his poetry. His poetry is very stark. Have you ever read any?"

"I must admit, I don't read a lot of poetry."

"Stephen says that's why civilization is dying, because people don't read poetry anymore."

"Could be," I said. I had my own theories on why civilization was dying, but they all took longer than a sentence to sum up.

"Matthew means 'gift of God,'" she informed me.

"More classics?"

"No, we thought we might have a child once, and we were discussing names, and we liked that one."

"My parents, too," I said. "Only they got the meaning mixed up. They thought it was *judgment* of God."

She laughed and told me I was wicked. I asked her where she wanted to eat. She told me that she would adore to get a burger at TGI Friday's.

"Interesting choice," I said.

"Why?"

"Because it's American, and because it's right around the corner from where Aliou got shot."

Phoebe said, "Ooh. Do you think we ought to pick another place?"

"No, now that you mention it, I could stand a burger myself."

Friday's wasn't too crowded. It was probably the most American place in London, not excluding the American embassy. It was dark, wood-lined, and multileveled, and decorated in the same miscellaneous-junk motif that marks all the branches of the chain (and of numerous competing chains) in the States.

More important, the food was the same. When you ordered something with ground beef, you got something recognizable as meat, not a fried-up version of stuff that had been macerated like baby food. The ice cream was real American-type ice cream, not the greasy, gritty stuff so common over here.

It didn't happen too often (every couple of weeks, or so), but any time Rox or I needed a jolt of home, we went to Friday's, and it was just like being back in the States. Until I went to the bathroom and tried to figure out how to flush the toilet.

The host at the door gave a little raised eyebrow as I walked in. He was used to seeing me with Roxanne.

Immune to vulgar curiosity, I asked for a nonsmoking table. We sat and ordered.

Friday's is a friendly place. The waiters and waitresses are encouraged to add eccentric customizations to their uniforms. They ask you where you're from. They ask you how everything is.

This is swell for the tourists, and the staff is (are, if you want to be British about it) bubbly and up and fun to talk to, if you don't have anything else to talk about. It can make conversation a little rough if you're trying to get information out of somebody.

I did manage to get a few words in and elicit a few replies.

Bristow's assistant, Detective Constable Griffiths, seemed to be a thorough, if uninspired, investigator. He'd done the whole routine, including asking most of the questions I'd asked myself.

"What *is* the point of that wretched English school?" she demanded. "They asked about it over and over."

"Aliou was killed trying to alert your—your what?—step-mother-in-law about that school. He must have found something about it he knew she'd be interested in. He knew the only reason he was hired to look around in the first place was that Lady Arking had gotten the anonymous letter."

"Maybe the broacher hid a secret message," she said.

I smiled. "Read a few thrillers in your time, haven't you?"

I was sorry the instant I said it. She drew back, and looked down at the plate where her barely nibbled-at hamburger lay.

"I'm sorry," she said. "I must seem awfully stupid to an expert. It was just an idea I had."

"Uh-huh," I said. "And it's just an idea *I* had, and it's just an idea *Scotland Yard* had. It's a very clever idea; it unfortunately just doesn't happen to be true."

"No?"

"They tried every test know to cryptoanalytic science. It's just a little cardboard folder about a one-flight-up school of English."

"Oh," Phoebe said. "Perhaps that explains why the police were so suspicious of us."

"How suspicious?"

"They even asked Stephen, Pamela, and me where we'd been Sunday night. Of course, we didn't know why at the time, but now we realize they suspect one of us of having killed that man who shot Aliou."

"What did you tell him?"

"I told him the whole thing was ridiculous."

"No, I mean where did you all tell him you were Sunday night?"

"Matt!" she breathed. "Not you too!"

"Relax," I told her. "Contrary to popular belief, that question does not indicate deep suspicion of the questionee. It's strictly routine."

She made a little moue of distaste. "It's routine for a *suspect.*

Pamela got so tense, I had to give her a neck massage after the police left."

"It's routine even before you know who's a suspect and who's not. Besides, it can be useful in other ways. If you know everybody's movements, you can work out the pattern the killer had to work his way through in order to commit the crime."

Phoebe's tiny mouth took another little nibble on her hamburger; she chewed thoroughly and swallowed, then patted a drop of ketchup off her pink lips with a napkin.

"What you just said sounds good," she told me when she was done, "but I don't think I actually understood it."

"Doesn't matter, it was mostly hot air anyway. Where were you Sunday night? See, when you're reluctant to answer that question, suspicion starts to creep in."

"I'm reluctant because I don't like the question, not because I'm ashamed of the answer."

"Strictly confidential," I promised.

"Oh, all right. I went to the cinema. The one on King's Road in Chelsea."

"What did you see?"

"*The Fugitive,*" she said. "You deduced yourself that I like thrillers."

"So I did. How'd you like it?"

"I thought it was marvelous. I'm quite a fan of Harrison Ford, as well."

"How did Stephen like it?"

"He didn't go. He was in his studio, working. That's what he's doing now, in fact. He's writing a play in verse; he says there hasn't been a good one since Shakespeare."

"I see," I said.

I already knew, because Bristow had mentioned it, that Lady Arking was accounted for, having spent half the time in question with Roxanne, and the other half on the phone with her solicitor.

I'd been slightly suspicious of that. The first murder I was ever involved in had to do with a fake phone alibi, and that was before mobile phones caught on the way they have today.

"Especially in London," I'd said. "You can't get on the damn bus without some teenager with a mobile phone sparking up his girlfriend and arranging to meet her at Knicker and Garter or some such place."

Bristow had wanted to know whose side I was on.

"Just the truth's," I told him. "It's only the truth that's going to get this business out of my life on a permanent basis."

He told me there was no cause to worry; cellular phone calls go through the system a completely different way from calls made on land lines, and there was a way to tell the difference.

"Not that it cuts a lot of ice in Lady Arking's case," he expanded, "since I don't really picture her personally putting three bullets at close range into Winston's chest. She's more the hiring type."

So, after a pleasant American lunch with Phoebe Arking, I more or less knew where the cops stood. For the English school angle, at least as it pertained to the Arkings, they had two nonalibis (it turned out that Stephen's studio had a private entrance to the street) and one ironclad alibi they couldn't care less about.

As far as the non-Arking angle went, they had only the immediate world.

So you could say the field was wide open.

Time for me to get around, get in the flow, see things with my own eyes. I find that often helps, even if the cops have already checked a place out thoroughly. I'm not a big intuition man, but feelings have their place when you're puzzling out a problem, and you might as well give them every chance.

"Sorry to be ungentlemanly," I told Phoebe, "but the time has come for me to put you in a cab and get to work."

"Oh, how very exciting. What are you going to do?"

"Nothing much," I said. "I thought I'd go and have a look at the

W. G. Peterson School of English. With luck, they may just take me for another cop."

I thought about it for a second and realized I was being a jerk. "No, they won't," I said, yanking my brain violently back from New York. "The minute I open my mouth, they'll know I'm an American."

"What are you going to do?" Phoebe asked. Her concern was all out of proportion to the problem.

I shrugged it off. "I'll think of something," I said. "I always do."

"Let me come with you," she said.

I knitted my brows and looked at her. "Why, for God's sake?"

"Oh, just to do something *mad* once. Stephen says true poetry is found on the edge of madness. I haven't done anything mad since . . ." She frowned, thinking it over.

Then the frown turned into a mischievous grin. "Since I rang Stephen out of the blue and told him how much I enjoyed his poetry." She put her hand on mine for a second. "There. You can't deny that worked out well, can you?"

"I suppose not," I conceded. "But this wouldn't be doing something mad. Not unless one of your definitions of 'mad' is 'boring.'"

"It's only boring to you because you do it all the time. All I ever do is type Stephen's poetry, go with Pamela to charity luncheons, and deal with the bank."

"See?" I said. "Don't sell your life short. I've never been to a charity luncheon. With or without Pamela."

"You're mocking me, but I don't care. I'll make a bargain with you. I'll bring you to our next charity luncheon if you'll take me along this afternoon."

Something had occurred to me. I didn't answer her right away because I was considering it.

"I won't be any bother," she said. "Not a bit of bother. I promise."

I looked at her and started to laugh. She got younger as I looked at her. Finally, when she reached about eight years old, she said, "Please?"

"Okay," I said.

She grabbed my hand in both of hers and squeezed. I got the impression that if I leaned forward an eighth of an inch, she'd vault the table and kiss me, and for the first time, I gave some credence to Roxanne's breakfast-time warning.

"But," I said sternly.

"Yes?"

"This is not a trip to the Barnes fete, okay? This is Yellowstone Park, and any creature may be a bear, and any bear may be hungry."

"I thought you said it would be boring."

"The overwhelming probability is that it will be. That doesn't change the fact that two men have already been shot to death in this mess, and we don't have the foggiest notion why. I know we're just going to Earl's Court—"

"Is that where we're going?"

"That's the place. And you and I both think we know Earl's Court. But any, repeat *any* community of humans is like an ants' nest. Take off the front wall and you never know what kind of activity you're going to find."

"Goodness," Phoebe said. "I thought only an artist like Stephen could get so intense."

"Still want to come?" Oops, I thought. Bad choice of words.

"Yes, I do," she said. "Very much so. I'll be a good girl and do whatever you say."

All of a sudden, the double entendres were flying so thick and fast, I was afraid to say anything for fear of incriminating myself. In my own eyes, if nowhere else.

I just said, "Fine," and dragged her out of there.

The cab struggled down Earl's Court Road, home of London's worst traffic, if you go by my experience of it. I had him drop us off in front of the Underground station, so we could come up to W. G. Peterson and his school slowly.

Earl's Court is one of London's more interesting neighborhoods. Unlike, say, Barnes, it actually behaves like a big-city neighborhood, going twenty-four hours a day, seven days a week.

Well, say eighteen hours a day. Even in Earl's Court, they don't want to overdo things.

Two kinds of people gravitate by some mystical process to the area—foreign students, of the full-time variety, not the visa-mill type; and Australians. In Earl's Court, you can purchase a magazine expressly for "Young Ozzies in London."

Another kind of industry seems to be centered in the Earl's Court area, though I couldn't prove it by personal experience. Walk into any phone booth in the area, and you'll see every available inch of space is covered by business cards sporting line drawings of women in various unorthodox attires, featuring most prominently garter belts or high, spike-heeled boots, carrying messages like "*HEADMISTRESS—knows how to deal with naughty boys*," followed by a phone number, or "Polly Morphus—discipline, bondage, enemas, you name it," also followed by a phone number. As we passed by a phone booth, I wondered idly what Phoebe would make of the cards.

I was familiar with Earl's Court for a totally different reason. Earl's Court Road was the home of, as far as I could tell, the one and only Taco Bell in the entire British Isles. Roxanne is afraid of what she thinks of as her addictive personality, but somehow, she let Taco Bell tacos crawl under her defenses.

She spotted the place one day, strictly by chance, from the top deck of the number 74 bus, and she almost caused a traffic pileup persuading the driver to make an unscheduled stop so she could get off the bus and get some. Now, every week or so, we have to make a run out here to stock up. She sogs them up in the microwave and eats them. She likes them soggy. I try not to look.

I was just as glad not to be going there today—it gets embarrassing ordering thirty tacos to go. Our destination was a couple of blocks past Taco Bell.

I saw the sign—one flight up, like all these places seemed to be, and about twenty yards ahead.

I stopped to speak to Phoebe. "All right, kid," I told her, "this is it."

She looked extremely alarmed. "This is what?" she wanted to know.

"This is your big chance at adventure. This is the private-eye caper you put in your memoirs."

"You're teasing me," she said.

"Little bit," I admitted. "But I'm not kidding about your being able to help me."

"You're not?"

"Cross my heart. It's not big, or very demanding, but it will help, if you do it."

"What do I have to do?"

"I'm going to go upstairs and tell a bunch of lies. All you have to do is stand next to me and act as if you believed them. If you managed to look demure and devoted, it would help the overall picture."

"What do I say?"

"After hello, nothing. I'll handle it. Remember, Jane Wyman won an Academy Award without saying a word."

"Don't you ever take anything seriously?"

"Sure," I said. "Everything. Except myself. It's the only path to true happiness."

"I'll try to remember that," she said.

The ground floor of the building held a newsagent's shop. Remembering the onion on my burger, I stopped in to get a roll of Trebor Soft Mints for my breath. I planned to lie to whomever I found inside; there was no reason to gross them out, too.

The *Evening Standard*, London's one and only afternoon news-paper, had come out. I took a quick look through it to see if Bris-tow had arrested anybody. He hadn't. The big news was some chicanery with a soccer player's contract, but that had been going on so long it was practically a soap opera.

"Okay," I told Phoebe outside, "here we go."

And in we went.

It wasn't exactly halls of ivy. The entryway looked like the back stairs of a very old hospital—clean enough, but shabby and gray. The stairs and railings were metal and concrete, painted over thickly in gray enamel. There were gray rubber treads on each step.

The door at the top of the stairs read "W. G. Peterson School of English, Fernando Weiskopf, Director."

I waited outside and listened. Phoebe started to say something, but I put a finger to my lips and she shushed.

If anybody was learning English inside there, it was happening very quietly. No talking, no lecturing, no sound of numerous peo-ple shuffling around in a classroom.

Not that it was completely silent, by any stretch of the imagina-tion. Drawers and doors were being opened and slammed, papers were being crumpled up, curses were being muttered.

It sounded suspiciously as if the place were being tossed by a none-too-competent and very frustrated searcher.

I took Phoebe by the shoulder. "Change of plan," I whispered. "You wait outside."

She pouted. "No," she whispered back.

So much for her promise, I thought. It wasn't really possible to argue, and pushing her down the stairs, while it would been very satisfying, was probably overkill. Also it would make too much noise.

"Wait halfway down the stairs then," I whispered. "I'll call you if everything is all right."

"Promise?"

"Yeah, just like you promised to listen to me, you miserable little twerp."

She grinned, kissed me on the nose, and retreated down the stairs as if she thought she was cute.

Cute my ass. When I'm about to go through a door with God knows what behind it, I don't want anybody playing games.

I waved Phoebe down a further couple of stairs, and she went reluctantly.

I tightened my lips and rolled my eyes. If Roxanne had ever had anything to worry about from this creature (which she had not) any vestige of it was gone by now.

I concentrated again on the door, and what might be behind it. I decided to do things the tried-and-true way.

I grabbed the knob, turned it quickly, and flung the door open.

I waited a second. There was no fusillade of gunfire, so I poked my head around.

A man sat at a desk, surrounded by piles of paper and plastic garbage bags full on the floor. He was dressed in a light blue suit, too summery for the weather. He had muddy blond hair, swarthy skin, and blue eyes. He was in his mid-to late-forties, slim, not too tall, and controlling his temper with an effort.

He fixed me with the blue eyes.

"I am sorry," he said. "We are not open."

He had a good voice, and spoke perfect English, but his accent was strange, as mixed up as his name was.

"That's okay," I said. "I just want to ask a few questions."

"*Journalists,*" he said. He said in the exact tone of voice you'd use if you found maggots in your peanut butter sandwich. "I have had too much of journalists."

"I'm not a journalist," I told him. "I'm a potential customer."

"Do you think I am an idiot? You are an American. You have no need of instruction. You speak English perfectly well. Unmusically perhaps, but perfectly comprehensibly."

"Thank you," I said. "I'm a potential customer, but not a potential student. The student would be Mathilde. She's a girl from the Dutch East Indies. We were lucky to find her. She's a great cook, and the children love her. She loves us, too, you see, or at least she says so, and she wants to stay in England. We all thought it would help if she learned English a little better, you know?"

I was going to go on to say that I'd understood that the school here was very understanding when it came to scheduling classes for the student when said student was free of other duties. I was going to add that Mathilde had an awful lot of other duties, and that there might be whole weeks when they didn't see her, but that of course did not reflect on her desire to learn the language, and that I would pay for the whole time the course took.

That's what I was *going* to tell him. The fact that I never got to certainly wasn't my fault, and after all the trouble I went to to concoct that lovely lie, I decided to put it down for you here, so it shouldn't go completely to waste.

The man behind the desk seemed to make an effort to get his agitation under control. He took a deep breath, and spread his hands in a conciliatory gesture.

"I'm sorry, sir, but the school is not accepting applicants at this time."

That was news to me. Bristow and boys had checked the place out, I knew. I wondered if the powers behind the school were running scared.

"Oh," I said. "That's a shame, Mr. . . . I presume you're Mr. Weiskopf?"

He bowed his head slightly.

"At your service," he smiled. Then his face fell. "Or, alas, not, since I have no services to offer at the present moment."

Unasked, I walked around to the front of his desk and took a seat, moving a stack of papers from the chair to do so. I tried to sneak a look at the papers, but they looked like authentic teachers' reports. I supposed they had to do *some* legitimate teaching around there, or at least fake it.

"Not at the present moment," I said.

"No, sir."

"If you'll forgive a personal comment, that's an interesting combination of names you have there."

"I am originally from Argentina, a nation of immigrants, no less than your own."

"True," I said. "And look at us now, here in London. We're turning England into a nation of immigrants, too. Of course, you know that; your business is built on it."

"Yes," he said sadly. Sad, he looked more Hispanic. "Yes, it was."

"Listen," I said. "How about a later moment?"

"I am afraid I don't understand."

I was a split second late in answering him; I'd caught something from the corner of my eye, a shape shifting on the other side of the pebbled glass of the doorway, on the landing in the hall.

You couldn't make out features, but the proportions and the colors were right. Phoebe had sneaked back upstairs to listen in. You'd think she would have had brains enough at least to have crouched down below the window and put her ear to the keyhole.

I couldn't figure out how Weiskopf couldn't see her. He had a better line of sight to the door than I did. Possibly, it was the fact that he was suddenly concentrating on my face as though he suspected me of something.

I didn't have enough spare brain cells to dwell on it at the moment. I was trying to think of something to do to Phoebe. A good spanking seemed appropriate, but Roxanne would misunderstand, and Phoebe, that perverse little twerp, would probably enjoy it.

"What don't you understand?" I asked Weiskopf. I found myself hoping I looked suspicious enough to keep his eyes focused on me and away from the door. I concentrated on averting my own gaze, so I wouldn't draw his attention to it.

"A later moment?"

"Oh, that. You said the school wasn't accepting pupils *at this time.* I was wondering when the next time would be that you *were* accepting students."

"Ah, I see," he said. "No, Mr. Cobb, it was a bad choice of words on my part. The school is closed indefinitely." A little of his old tension and anger came back. "The school may well be no more."

I was horrified.

"But *why?*" I demanded. "I've heard such good things about this place."

"It is truly sad," Weiskopf said. "But events beyond my control have made it impossible to continue. I have already made the faculty redundant. You come upon me in the midst of cleaning out the office for the last time."

"What kind of events?" I asked, thinking the answer ought to be good, like "One of our students got wasted the other night," or something along those lines.

But it turned out to be even better than that.

He said, "We have been driven from business by the power of lies and false publicity."

Then he said, "What is the matter?"

This last question let me know my face had slipped. I decided it didn't matter anyway.

"You like that line, don't you?" I said.

"Again, Mr. Cobb, I'm afraid I don't understand."

"The stuff about lies and false publicity. You used it word for word in the anonymous letter you sent to Lady Arking.

Weiskopf's face went completely blank. Right now, he didn't look German *or* Hispanic. He just looked dead.

"You are talking nonsense," he said. "You will go now."

"I don't think so," I said. "Especially since you've called me Cobb twice since I've been here."

"So? That is your name, is it not?"

"Sure it's my name, but *I* haven't mentioned it. What is it? Did you recognize me from the papers or the TV news? I got a decent amount of publicity on Monday."

Weiskopf didn't answer, so I answered myself.

"Nah," I said. "That can't be it. At least not all of it, because there was no reason for you not to have said something about it. You're hiding something, Weiskopf."

"I am hiding nothing, except the depth of my anger at you for disrupting an already sad day with your lies."

"Yeah," I said. "And false publicity, I know. Listen, what I think we're going to do here is call Detective Inspector Bristow, and have him come down here with some of his men and help you clean out the office."

"I do not have to stand for this!"

"I think you probably do. I'm fifteen years younger, five inches taller, and fifty pounds heavier than you. I don't think you're going to get through me. May I use your phone, please?"

So much for my tough-guy act. He picked the damn thing up and threw it at me.

It was a modern phone—light plastic and microchips. Considering the force with which it hit me in the face, if it had been one of the old-fashioned Bakelite-and-metal jobs, it would have killed me.

As it was, it tied me up just long enough for him to make a break for the door.

As I pulled phone cord from around my neck, I yelled "Phoebe! Get the hell out of there!"

Quick, clicking footsteps on the stairs showed me that for once, to my astonishment, she had actually listened.

I got loose and took off after the Argentine Flash. He was about halfway down the stairs when I got through the door. He was too far away for me to launch myself in a flying tackle that way PC Staines got me, but I swear I got down the stairs without my feet having touched the rubber treaders more than twice.

I left my fingerprints on the fabric of his jacket, but I slipped on the welcome mat and lost my grip. He disappeared out the door.

Goddammit, I thought, even as I was scrambling to my feet, how embarrassing this was going to be when I had to tell Bristow about it.

I was tempted to just lie there and let him go, except I had visions of Phabulous Phoebe trying to stop him on her own, or worse, of Weiskopf grabbing her and holding her hostage to make good his escape.

In retrospect, I realize what a goop I was. I had no legal standing whatsoever. All Weiskopf had done was to flee from a maniac who had announced his intention to hold him captive in his own office.

I didn't have a single witness who could back up the fact that the Argentinian liked to quote from unpublished anonymous letters, or that he'd called me by my name without ever having heard it.

Or maybe I did. Who knows what Phoebe managed to gather, hanging around outside the door. Maybe she did put her ear to the keyhole for a while.

I, however, was not thinking of any of that at the time. I just wanted to get out the door, and see if I could at least determine the direction he went in.

That's when he got me again. The next time I pick somebody to bully, I'll be more careful about it.

Because the clever son of a bitch hadn't run away at all. He was waiting just past that inner door, in the vestibule, and he kicked me a good one in the nuts as I came through the door.

I said something like *"Ooooooooooooooooooo,"* and fell to my knees on the tile floor. Weiskopf kicked me again, in the stomach this time. They must play lots of soccer in Argentina. I think the only reason he didn't kill me was insufficient space to wind up.

He said, "*Auf Wiedersehen*, Mr. Cobb," and walked off, laughing softly.

I'd like to think he was still laughing when he stumbled off the curb and got run over by the taxi.

# 14

**"We must apologize to our deaf viewers for the loss of subtitles."**

Angela Rippon
*Evening News,* BBC

/t all happened in the few seconds it took me to stagger to my feet and come out of the building nursing my Grievous Bodily Harm. The squeal of breaks and the screams of passersby hadn't died away yet.

A crowd had gathered already, but I was tall enough to see over the top of it, and one look was enough.

Weiskopf was dead. No one gets a London taxi parked on his head and lives.

It would have made me queasy if I weren't already queasy from being kicked in the balls and the gut. My sentiments toward Weiskopf, had I been pressed to put them into words at that moment, would have been, "Serves the bastard right." Uncharitable of me, perhaps, but anybody who's gotten a kick like that will understand. Everybody else will just have to take my word for it.

The stars Weiskopf had made me see were drifting out of my field of vision, and my brain was beginning to clear. The first thing that came to me was Phoebe. Where the hell was Phoebe?

Silly question. Phoebe was right where I'd expect her to be, in the very front of the crowd, gaping at the stiff with her little mouth hanging open, close enough to get blood on her darling little pumps if she stepped six inches off the curb.

I snaked an arm through the mass of bodies and caught hold of the strap of her shoulder bag. At the same time, I said her name, gently but firmly. The last thing I needed at a time like this was to be busted as purse snatcher.

"Phoebe?" I said. "Phoebe?"

I was pulling on the strap, but she wouldn't move.

*"Phoebe!"* I barked, and she jumped and looked at me.

With an incredible effort of will, I forced myself to smile and not to scream.

Keeping a gentle traction on the strap, I pulled her through the crowd, all the while talking gently.

"Phoebe," I said. "Come along, dear. We don't want to be morbid, do we?"

She goddamn well *did* want to be morbid, but by a combination of a continued pull on the bag and the wedging action of the more unabashedly morbid who were edging into the space Phoebe had occupied, I finally managed to get her free with only a single wistful backward glance.

Still pulling her by the bag strap, I led her down the street and around the corner. I did not do the more natural thing and take her hand, because I was afraid if I laid a finger on her, I would strangle her.

A couple of blocks up the street, Earl's Court was deserted. Naturally. Even the Headmistress and her naughty clients had to roll out to see this. I felt it safe to vent a few of my feelings.

*"What the hell's the matter with you?"* I hissed.

Phoebe said nothing. Her face started to cloud up. Another hundredth of an inch fall in her emotional barometer, and she would start to cry.

*William L. DeAndrea*   **138**

I realized I was still holding the strap of her bag, and for the first time I also realized something else. The bag was heavy all out of proportion to its size.

"This thing weighs a ton," I said. "What have you got in here, a brick?"

I took it off her to look inside. I don't know why I did. To distract myself from the anger and frustration that were about to explode me into a bigger mess than Weiskopf now was, maybe. Maybe because it was one mystery about this mess that had a solution right to hand.

Anyway, I took the bag, into which a brick might just about have fit, opened it, and found the gun.

This was no toy gun, either. This was a no-nonsense blue steel, American-made Hopkins & Allen .38 caliber Police Special, loaded (a quick look at the cylinder told me) with actual bullets.

"Phoebe!"

"Yes, Matt?"

"For God's sake, what is this? And if you tell me it's a gun, I swear I'm going to slug you one."

"You wouldn't do that," she said confidently. "You're a gentleman, American or not."

I counted to ten in four languages, took a deep breath, and said as calmly as I could, "Why are you packing a rod, Phoebe?"

She smiled. "I like that," she said. "It makes me feel like a moll. Do you still call them molls?"

"I don't call them anything. Listen, Phoebe, try to relate to something back here on Planet Earth. I more or less just chased a man to his death, okay? I would very much like to know what the hell is going on in my life. Are you with me so far?"

"Of course I am. Sometimes people treat me as if I had no sense at all. I think it's because I'm little. But I am a fully mature married woman, you know."

"I know, I know. The gun?"

"Stephen gave it to me. Made me take it, really. He said with the situation the way it is, there was a small but real chance I might be in danger. So he wanted me to be able to protect myself."

"Do you have a license for this thing?"

"I don't know," she said. "Stephen might. Do I need one?"

Actually, I didn't know the answer to that myself, though I strongly suspected she did need one, based on how the British papers ran distraught editorials at least once a day on how lax American gun laws were.

"I'll keep this," I said. I slipped it into my pocket.

"All right," she said, "but you don't have a license for it either."

"I'll risk it. Tell me what happened out on the street. No. Tell me what happened after you came back upstairs."

She looked surprised. "Nothing, really. I felt stupid waiting halfway up the stairs, so I came up."

Of course, it never occurred to her to go the rest of the way downstairs, the way I wanted her to in the first place.

I could hear sirens from around the corner. Ambulance, cops, didn't matter. Time to make this quick and get out of there.

"Did you hear anything of our conversation?" I asked.

"No," she pouted. "And it wasn't from lack of trying, either. I strained to hear. I did everything but put my ear to the keyhole."

"Phoebe," I said, "I hope you enjoyed your afternoon. From now on stay out of the investigations business."

"I didn't hear anything," she went on, "until you called to me to run away."

"Okay, you ran away. Where did you go?"

"Just outside the building, on the pavement. I—I didn't know where to go."

"That part was fine. He had no reason to recognize you. What happened next?"

"Nothing for the longest time. I was worried about you."

Actually, it had been about thirty seconds, but it had seemed like the longest time to me, too. Now, with a dull ache in my loins and an acute case of trauma-induced indigestion, I felt as if it were still going on.

"Thank you."

"Then he came out of the building. He was a bit disheveled, but he was laughing. He was looking back at the building. I'd come around to the edge of the pavement by then, hoping to get a look into the vestibule, when he walked right by me. He was fixing his cravat, you know, looking up into the air the way men do. At least, Stephen does it that way. And laughing, he was still laughing."

Phoebe made a helpless little shrug.

"And then . . . and then without knowing it, he stepped off the curb, stumbled and fell into the road. And the taxi came by—it couldn't stop in time. There was a crunch and a splash—it was horrible."

"I'm sure it was," I told her. "Here's what I want you to do. Let me put it this way. I'm about to ask you to do something. Please, please, *please* just *do* it, okay? No matter how many better ideas you have."

Her eyes opened until they were nearly as wide as her eyeglass frames.

"All you have to do is tell me," she insisted. "You're the boss. That's what we agreed. Don't worry about being forceful with me, Matt. I admire that in a man. Forcefulness is very . . . male."

God spare me, I thought. "Okay," I said. "I'm being forceful. Go home. Sit there. Read a book. Watch the telly. Read today's *Orbit*. Don't phone anybody to tell them your big adventure. Don't interrupt Stephen to tell him. Let him do his best for Shakespeare in peace."

"I can't tell anyone?"

"Not till you hear from me."

Her voice went all warm and gooey. "Am I going to hear from you, Matt?"

I ignored her. "The police. If the police come to you and tell you about this, tell them the truth. Answer all their questions."

"I'm tired of answering their questions."

Dealing with Phoebe was like fighting Marshmallow Fluff (which is available in England, by the way)—no matter how hard you hit it, it didn't get hurt, and you were stuck all the worse.

"Force yourself," I said.

The eyes were still round. "Matt," she said. "This has been the most exciting day of my life."

"You're young yet," I told her.

She thought that over for a second, then said, "Matt? It would be mad for us to have a . . . a fling, wouldn't it?"

"Mad," I said, "doesn't begin to describe it."

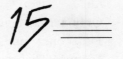

## 15

**"I don't think much of the platform."**

**"Well, it's my party."**

**"And you'll cry if you want to."**

Tony Cannon and Bobby Ball
*Cannon & Ball*, ITV

*I* finally got home about ten o'clock at night.

"Thank you," I told Roxanne when she greeted me at the door.

She gave me a kiss and said, "What for?"

"The only reason Bristow did not throw me back in the clink was that he was afraid of what you'd do to get me out of there this time."

"What happened?"

I told her about my adventures in Earl's Court.

She showed me a grin of triumph. "I told you, huh? Didn't I? I knew she was after your bod."

Then she frowned. "Your *bod!*" she said. "Take off your clothes."

"Roxanne, for God's sake!"

She rolled her eyes. "Nothing wrong with your ego, is there? Yes, Cobb, I do find you irresistible, but I'm not about to ravish you right here. Get the clothes off."

I was still suspicious. "What for?"

"You've been, as the English would put it, ill used, haven't you?"

"I'll say."

"All right then. Consider this a study into the feasibility of future ravishments."

"Ah."

"Or do I mean ravishings?"

"Either one sounds good to me."

"Mmmm. Then you can't be too badly hurt."

I agreed, but she went ahead and checked me out.

"Nice bruise on the abdomen," she said. "Looks like a map of Australia."

"Don't mention Australia. It reminds me of Earl's Court."

She touched me. "Does that hurt?"

"No, actually. It feels pretty good."

"Cobb, I swear you could get aroused by a navel orange."

"Only if it was your navel orange," I said staunchly.

"Okay, no swelling—"

"No?"

"No *abnormal* swelling, okay? Have you gone to the bathroom since this happened?"

"Couple of times. Learned how to work three new kinds of toilets."

"Urine look okay? Not cloudy or dark?"

"No, doctor, it looked the way it usually looks. How do you know to ask me all this stuff?"

"At one point, during the time you were wasting your life with lesser women, I took a notion that I might want to be a doctor."

"Why did you decide against it?"

"You could never count on a day off."

"Can I get dressed now?"

"If you must. I think you're going to be okay, but I wish you'd see a regular doctor. After all, it's free."

She laughed. We'd already had a few experiences with socialized medicine.

"And worth every penny of it," I said.

"Well, it is if you can't afford anything else," she said.

"And if you don't smoke," I said. The papers were full recently of a man who was refused necessary heart treatment because he smoked. The other big recent NHS stories included a woman on the dole and her boyfriend who were given fertility treatments so they could bring a sextuplet of little mouths to the public trough, and thousands of people who were told they had cancer when they didn't.

"Our doctor is good," Rox said.

"True. I'll see him tomorrow."

As I slid back into my sweats and T-shirt for hanging around the house, Rox asked me, "So why did Bristow want to throw you back in jail?"

"Shucks," I said. "Got me. All I did was horn in on the closest thing he had to a suspect, or even a lead, and provoke the guy into killing himself. Then, a half hour later, I turn up in a cab with an unlicensed gun in my pocket to tell him I'm sorry, and he takes offense. How do you figure that?"

She shook her head sadly. "Some people are just touchy, I guess."

"Mmmm," I said. "Guess so. Seriously, though, it's not as bad as it sounds."

"It's not? How?"

"He had a big mystery on his hands—why did Weiskopf go striding, laughing like a maniac, out of his office in the middle of the afternoon, with his packing still left undone? I solved that one for him at least. And I brought him information, even if I cut off a source of actual evidence."

"What do you mean?"

"Weiskopf wrote the anonymous letter. That connects him with the start of the investigation. The brochure connects the school—and by extension Weiskopf—with Aliou. He keeps turning up, you see."

*Killed in the Fog*   **145**

Roxanne bit her lip. "I know this is probably horrendously dumb in some obvious way, but has it crossed anybody's mind that it might have been Weiskopf who did the killings?"

"It has," I said. "Bristow was working on it even before today's little unpleasantness. He'd already found out a lot about the guy."

"Such as?"

"To start with the most suspicious circumstance, Weiskopf had an alibi for Sunday afternoon, when Winston was killing Aliou, but no alibi for Sunday night when Winston was getting his."

"That's the way it would work if he were guilty, right?"

"That's why that's the most suspicious thing. His background is interesting, too. He was the son of a Nazi who fled Germany after the war. The old man wasn't a war criminal, or at least, he wasn't wanted for anything. He just decided he'd find more congenial company in the Argentine. Weiskopf came to England in 1977, to study at Cambridge."

Rox was surprised. "That's a piss-poor job he had, for a Cambridge graduate."

"He didn't graduate. He flunked out, or was quietly kicked out for cheating—something like that. Bristow's still got men working on it. He was about to lose his student visa, but he married a waitress, and was granted landed emigrant status."

"What happened to the wife?"

"Divorced about a year after Weiskopf got permission to stay. Ex-wife died about five years ago. She really *did* have cancer. No kids. Turns out, Weiskopf had a bit of form, as they say here."

"A what?"

"A criminal record."

"That's interesting. What did he do?"

"Public disturbances, things like that. In 1982, during the Falklands War. He started an organization called 'Justice for the Malvinas.' I think, like Lee Harvey Oswald and his Fair Play for Cuba Committee, Weiskopf was the founder and only member.

"Still, he got some ink—Bristow showed me a big story from the *Orbit*—and made himself drastically unpopular. I saw the file. Some enthusiast at the Yard considered the possibility of arresting him for treason, but somebody senior (and with more sense) said that would be giving him infinitely more publicity than he deserved. He tried to make it as a writer—essays, plays, poems, whatever."

"Maybe Stephen could have helped him," Rox said with a smile.

"Maybe so," I agreed. "He certainly could have used the help. He was on the dole for a couple of years in the late eighties. No record of his ever actually publishing anything."

"Then, in 1990, he bought the W. G. Peterson School of English and installed himself as headmaster."

"How did he do that if he was on welfare?" Rox asked.

I shrugged. "Part of it came from a grant; the rest, who knows? I don't suppose it's easy to save money on the dole, but if you live alone, it shouldn't be impossible. Maybe he borrowed money from a friend. Maybe he had a good tip on a horse race."

"Maybe," Roxanne suggested, "his father had told him the secret location of a missing hoard of Nazi gold and art treasures."

I nodded. "There you go. That's undoubtedly it. He just suffered through years of penury to make it look good later."

"Sounds good to me," Rox said.

"Dollink," I told her, "sometimes living with you is like living with Tom Sawyer."

"I'll take that as a compliment."

"That's how I meant it. Anyway," I went on, "there is no remaining doubt that the school in question was in fact a visa mill. Bristow had been tracking down former students, promising to straighten things out with the Home Office if they'd talk."

"Can he do that?" she wondered.

"Sure," I said. "He can make promises all day. As for actually getting legit long-term visas for them, that I don't know."

"This is such an unpleasant business, sometimes," she said.

I sighed. "I know, my love. That's why I tried to get out of it, remember?"

"Dimly," she said. "Well, we had it going pretty good there for a couple of months."

"We will again, after this is cleared up," I promised.

"We'll try. Sometimes, though, I think you can't fight Fate."

"You can fight it," I said. "I do it all the time. Sometimes it seems that that's practically all I do."

"How often do you win?"

"Often enough. I'm here with you, am I not? What were the odds against that?"

"Good point," she said. "While we're talking about odds, what are the odds that the case is already cleared up?"

"You mean that Weiskopf was the killer, and the Crown doesn't have to shell out for a trial or incarceration because he so considerately offed himself?"

"Yeah," she said. "That's what we were talking about."

"Well, even though Bristow and I would dearly love that to be the case, I have to say that the odds are tiny that Weiskopf was it."

Rox seemed offended. "Why not?" she demanded. "He was weird enough. He was sleazy enough. He was smart enough. He was ruthless enough."

"How do you know he was ruthless enough?"

"He beat you up, didn't he?"

I got up on my machismo. "I just like to think that proves he was *sneaky* enough."

"That still adds up to a possible killer, doesn't it?"

"That much does," I said. "But not the rest."

"The rest of what?"

"The rest of what we know about him."

"So tell me the rest," she said, "and we'll see."

I shook my head. "It's nothing you don't know already. Look, Weiskopf was a maniac, but he wasn't an idiot. He knew the jig was up, and he cleaned out as many incriminating documents as he could, but he wasn't in a panic about it. He didn't torch the building. He'd taken plenty of money out of that place, and no doubt he was planning to go to wherever he'd stashed it and spend the rest of his life with it, with or without a stay in prison first."

"I don't get it."

"Look. Weiskopf is running a very illegal and very profitable business. He comes under some suspicion, then passes through the first waves of publicity relatively unscathed. What does he do now? He writes an anonymous letter to Lady Arking, getting at least one newspaper back investigating in a serious way. I've got to admit, I *still* can't figure that part of it out. Like I said, he was at least part maniac.

"Still. He's got the investigation going. Joseph Aliou somehow gets around to him, and he gets on to Joseph Aliou. Whom he has killed, for investigating what Weiskopf practically gave him an engraved invitation to investigate. It'd almost be like Weiskopf was setting himself up so that he *had* to murder somebody."

"That's not very smart, is it?"

"No. It's idiotic. Especially when there's no reason on earth for it. That kind of behavior is likely to end you up dead."

"Which it did," Roxanne pointed out.

"No," I said. "*Some* chain of events ended him up dead, but we don't know just what yet. This theory makes no sense. Especially when you consider that I walk into the room and he quotes the anonymous letter for me. Remember, he knew who I was. If he'd been hiding knowledge of the murders of Aliou and Winston, I doubt he would have quoted his anonymous letter, consciously or unconsciously."

"So he *didn't* do it."

"Got me," I said. "But if he did do it, it's one of those maddening things in life that will never make any sense. I try not to accept those until I have to."

"Cobb's razor."

I grinned. "I never thought of it that way before. Kind of makes me see myself in a whole new light."

"So what do we do now?" she asked.

The whole new light flickered and died. "Go to bed, I guess. I'm tired. How did your day go, by the way?"

"Pretty well," she said. "I gave an abstract on my paper of American imports of medical supplies from Britain, 1860 to 1865, and they actually listened. Some of them. Why is it easier to answer intelligent questions than stupid ones?"

Being an intelligent question, that one was easy to answer. "Because," I said, "when somebody asks you a stupid question, you have to educate them to a certain level before they can even understand an answer."

On that note of intellectual triumph, we went to bed, where, to our mutual surprise, we scored a couple of physical triumphs and more or less decided a trip to the doctor tomorrow would be superfluous.

Then the phone rang. It was Stephen Arking.

"Cobb," he said. "I understand you spent the day with my wife. I think we should have a little talk."

# 16

Stephen was less than forthcoming on the phone.

When I hung up Roxanne said, "What was that all about?"

"Not sure," I told her. "My best guess is that Phantastic Phoebe told him some sort of story."

"Oh no."

"And now he wants to challenge me to a duel."

"Right," she said. "Swords or pistols?"

"Neither. Dirty limericks at ten yards. First one who cracks up laughing loses. Although I'd consider honor satisfied with a snicker."

"You're doomed," she said.

"What do you mean? I know more dirty limericks than anybody. 'There was a young fellow from Kent—'"

"I like that one," she said. "But that's not the point. I don't know Stephen very well, but my impression of him is that he's not the type to laugh at dirty limericks. He might not even be the type to *get* dirty limericks. And even if he did, he would hate them as insults to Poetry."

"You're probably right," I said. "I'm doomed. I'll switch to pistols. After all, I'm an American. We're gun-toting, bloodthirsty killers one and all, right? I mean, if you read the English papers. Geez, now I'm sorry I gave the pistol I got from Phoebe to Bristow."

"Seriously, Cobb, what are you going to say to him?"

"Seriously, Rox, I don't know. I'll probably tell him his wife is certifiable, and I don't even know how *he* manages to sleep with her, let alone me."

"Oh, that'll make him feel better."

"My love," I said sincerely, "I am too tired to care. Let's get some sleep."

"You sleep, love," she told me. "I'm going be up all night; I'm going to get some steel wool and knit you a bulletproof vest."

I dreamed about that damned bulletproof vest. It occurred to me that Americans had the reputation, but it was the English who were slinging the hardware in this case. Assuming an Englishman had killed Winston, of course.

Assuming further that Phoebe had been telling the truth (a risky proposition, to be sure), I was going to spend the morning talking to a man who had had access to at least one illegal gun. I think my subconscious had decided that a bulletproof vest, even a homemade one, was a good idea.

I woke up mumbling, "But what if it rains?"

Roxanne was lying beside me, snoring softly. For once I managed to get out from under the hand she inevitably placed in the middle of my chest without waking her. I took a shower and got dressed. She hadn't actually knitted the vest, so I decided to go as I was.

I left her a note and took off.

It was a lousy day for a duel. It was cold, overcast, and even snowing a little. People were talking about it. The first November snow in London for twenty-four years, they said.

I was glad I hadn't missed it.

I got to Stephen's studio just about the appointed hour of ten o'clock. This was the top floor of the Kensington house. As Phoebe had said, there was a separate entrance, so I didn't have to run the risk of running into her and adding to whatever offenses I'd already committed.

I rang the bell down in the street and got buzzed in. Stephen was waiting for me at the top of the stairs, looking especially Byronic with a strand of hair across his forehead and white silk shirt open at the collar.

He looked ready for a duel, but he made no mention of one. Didn't indicate any hostility. He shook my hand and offered me a drink; when I told him it was a little too early for me, he grinned.

"I live on my own private clock, I'm afraid, here in my little snuggery. I've been at work for six hours already, so I will indulge, if you don't mind."

"Not at all."

"Meanwhile, may I offer you some coffee or tea?"

"I'd like some tea," I said.

"Won't be a minute," he said, and went around a partition to a kitchenette. "Make yourself at home."

I looked around the place. I didn't know if Stephen was much of a poet (though I soon found out), but I admired his taste in snuggeries. If he'd designed the place himself, I decided, he was more of an artist than even Phoebe thought.

It was just a large, comfortable room, with lots of big chairs and comfortable sofas and cushions. There was even a big, solid-looking rocking chair, the first one I'd seen in England after three months of assiduous looking.

One wall was curtained windows, one was a desk with a word-processor screen glowing green-on-gray on top of it, and the other two were bookshelves.

As an incurable and unabashed bookshelf snoop, I took a look. Poetry. All the classics, from the English tradition and in translation, but most of it was contemporary. Acres and acres of it. It occurred to me that if Stephen actually read all this, no wonder he was on a different time scheme from the rest of humanity.

It also occurred to me that he was undoubtedly the only one in the world who had bought copies of even half this stuff.

There was a good shelf full of the works of Stephen Arking, bound in blue leather, stamped in gold.

As I was beginning to learn (and to warn myself about) having money in the family could make virtually everything in life nicer.

Stephen seemed to be taking an awfully long time over a cup of tea. I wondered if anything had happened to him. Then I realized what was going on. A guy who had enough money to have his poetry bound in leather and gold leaf could undoubtedly afford a screen saver for his computer. A quick look at the wiring setup showed me that Stephen did. The fact that it was not in use implied that he wanted me to see what was on the screen.

I thought of ignoring it, to see how long he'd wait before giving up, but I decided against it. I'd come here after all to talk to the man, not to drive him nuts.

I went to the screen and read.

> *In orgasmic ecstasy,*
> *I plied my blade*
> *Heedless of resistance*
> *Of supplicant hand*
> *Of cowered posture*
> *Of bone, of flesh,*

*I swung*
*And swung and swung*
*Till no "he" remained*
*Bits only, unrecognizable*
*Is this a head?*
*No more. A half.*
*Brainless*
*A bowl to retch in*
*I said Good I*
*Rested content.*

*Jesus,* I thought. I remembered that whole shelf of books, presumably filled with stuff like that, and suppressed a shudder. I mean, I knew poetry was dead, but this was dancing on the grave.

Stephen came back in with the tea.

"I brought, cream, sugar, and lemon, since I don't know how you take it."

"Thanks," I said. I sat down next to the table on which he had put the tea, and started adding cream and sugar.

"What do you think?" he asked.

"What about?"

"No need to be coy. I saw you at the computer screen."

I thought I liked my tea sweet, but this guy was ridiculous. After about seven spoonfuls of sugar, he took a sip, made a face, and added another. "You must have read my current opus in progress. What do you think?"

I managed a sheepish grin. "I didn't mention it, because I didn't know if you'd mind."

He waved off any concern. "Just a little test to see how curious a guest is." Which was a lie. If I hadn't read that screen, he'd still be out in the kitchen futzing around with the tea.

"And," he went on, "to get feedback on my work, you see. The audience for good poetry these days is, ah, shall we say . . . select?"

Shall we say . . . extinct? Along with good poetry? I have a reputation as a nice guy, but only because my mouth is more disciplined than my brain.

"I've decided that anyone curious enough to read the screen will be perceptive enough to have a useful opinion."

"Interesting reasoning," I said.

He leaned forward, arms and legs both crossed in the defensive yet somehow vulturelike pose made famous by Sir David Frost.

"So, what's yours?" he asked.

"Oh, the tea will be fine."

He was haughtily amused. "No, dear boy. What's your useful opinion of the *poem?*"

I was trapped now.

I pursed my lips for a moment and said, "It's *powerful.*"

That was not a lie. So is ipecac.

It made Stephen's day. He unwound himself and clapped, applauding either my perception or his own brilliance, it was hard to tell.

"That was the effect I was striving for. Editors at the journal say it's *too* powerful for them, but I refuse to soften my work. One's art must not be subject to compromise, don't you agree?"

As a matter of fact, I did. I told him so.

"I am fortunate enough to have been provided for by my father—not lavishly, but comfortably. My stepmother keeps the level of support artificially low because she still hopes to drive me into the family business. Not to denigrate the news or anything, but nothing can be further from my interests.

"You see, what Pamela doesn't understand is that one's muse is a much more demanding boss than any of you . . . *television* executives could ever be. I'm sure *you* at least, can understand that."

"I don't know," I said. "We are not a muse."

He frowned, then mumbled, "We are not a . . . Oh! Excellent, Cobb, excellent. As you undoubtedly noticed, I'm not averse to a bit of the old paranomasia myself. Did you like the double meaning—'cowered' and 'coward'?"

"Daring," I said.

He shrugged. "How can there be Art without daring?" My assumption that the question was rhetorical turned out to be correct, and, boy, was I glad.

"But, dear boy," he went on. "I'm being selfish. I didn't ask you out here to talk about my poetry."

It was nice to have that stated categorically. I was beginning to wonder.

"We're here to talk about my wife."

He sat there looking at me. It went on for a long time. I kept looking for something other than bland good-fellowship, but I never found it.

That was somehow more unsettling than outright hostility would have been.

"Quite a gal," I ventured.

"Yes indeed," he said. "Underneath that bone-china exterior is the spirit of adventure that made the Empire. Or so they tell me. Absolutely devoted to me and my art; builds her life around my poetry. Have I mentioned she handles all the tedious secretarial and accountancy chores for this household?"

"I think you have, yes, the other night at your stepmother's."

"Well, she does. You don't know what a relief it is to a chap never to worry about money. Or, ha-ha, maybe you do."

I looked into that nudge-nudge, wink-wink smile, and I swore to myself never to budge an inch on the issue of the prenuptial agreement. I smiled back, a little wearily. "I was eating regular before I ever met Roxanne Schick," I said.

"Of course you were. Look at the size of you. No wonder Phoebe is smitten with you."

"I beg your pardon?"

"Come, come, Cobb. We're all adults here, aren't we? All I'm saying is, next time, take the poor girl to a decent hotel instead of dragging her into dangerous criminal things. She might have been hurt, and I couldn't live without her, for all that I spend too much time with the muse. I am totally fulfilled in my work, eh? But Phoebe must have her outlet, too. I don't mind, especially when she shows such excellent taste."

It takes a lot to get me sputtering, but this did it. "Wait a minute—you think I—she—that I—what the hell did she *tell* you?"

"That you arranged an assignation, but went off on this case business, and the fellow got careless and got himself killed, and you never got around to *doing* anything, poor children."

"*I have no sexual interest in your wife!*"

"Now, I know America is still a Puritan country, my boy, but there's really no need to keep up appearances. Phoebe and I are beyond all that."

"Puritan, my ass! Phoebe and you are both nuts. Where did you get that gun?"

"Gun?"

"The unlicensed gun I took away from her yesterday afternoon. The one you gave her to protect herself." I shivered in retrospect. "God," I said, "the idea of either one of you maniacs with a gun is enough to make me want to paste hundred-dollar bills to myself and run naked through Times Square. I'd feel safer."

"Cobb, there's no need to introduce extraneous topics like guns into a civilized conversation. If you're uncomfortable with my knowing, forget I ever said a word. Carry on as you've been. I daresay it'll add a bit of spice for Phoebe."

"You and Phoebe," I said, "deserve each other. I am leaving. I will deal, henceforth, through Lady Arking. Get out of my way."

"Does this mean you won't be calling Phoebe?"

I stormed downstairs, hailed a cab and went home. I was still storming when I walked in. Rox looked up at me with questioning eyes.

"*Pack!*" I screamed.

*17* ≡≡≡

We didn't pack, much as I wanted to at that moment.

For one thing, I think that particular trick would have torn Bristow's nose clean off his face. He wasn't too pleased with me at the moment as it was, and an attempt to leave the country might well provoke an international incident.

For another thing, I was goddamn mad.

"I," I told my sweetheart some hours later when she'd managed to calm me down a little, "am goddamn mad."

"At who, precisely?" she asked.

"Whom," I corrected automatically.

"Whoa," she laughed. "You are mad. When you start giving me that English major crap, you are on the boil."

"I wouldn't mention it under ordinary circumstances," I said, "but I want you to make a good impression on these professors and things you hang around with."

"You mean like you, when you told Professor Manders you were convinced he dropped his accent and talked regular when there were no Americans around.

"He laughed."

"Yeah. He laughed. *I* almost died. Have a scone."

"Good idea." I split the scone open and spooned some rich, thick clotted cream on top, with an artistic red drop of strawberry jam in the middle. This creation, especially the cream, was in itself an argument for staying in England.

We were sitting at a massive, scarred wooden table in the kitchen, with the booty of the pantry and the fridge spread before us. Rox knew me well enough to know that I'd get calmer as I got fuller.

I said something in a little spray of crumbs.

"Swallow what you've got," Roxanne suggested, "and try again."

I washed it down with a big glug of creamy English milk. "I'm still mad," I said.

"At whom?" she asked, then ruined it by adding, "Not meem, I hope."

I wasn't being bitter, just stating facts, when I said. "No. Practically everybody but youm, as a matter of fact. At the world. At Fate."

"We were talking about Fate yesterday."

"I know. Mostly, though, I'm mad at myself. For going down to TVStrato in the first place. For getting sucked into this mess. But mostly for being so damned *bad* at it."

One of the things that makes Rox tops in the girlfriend department is that she's always ready to spring to my defense, even when I'm the one attacking me.

"What do you mean, bad?"

"Aliou got murdered in front of my eyes."

"Your back was turned, and you couldn't help it. And you were the only one who saw the real killer at all."

"Who I failed to catch. Whom."

"Because you were tackled by that policeman."

"Who caught me from behind. Then I get a bright idea and a break, and I flush a figure who knows *something* about the mess, and before I can call the cops not only does he beat the snot out of me, he then proceeds to get conveniently killed so nobody can ask him any questions."

"Who might even be the killer, for all you know."

"Exactly. For all I know. For all anyone will ever know. If this all goes on too long without an answer, you know Bristow will just chalk it up to Weiskopf—I won't blame him, he'll have to do it— but that'll leave the real killer out there, laughing.

"And talk about laughing. In consecutive days, I let myself be made a fool of by two of the biggest twits imaginable. That idiot Stephen actually thinks I'm having it off with Phoebe, and he's grateful for the favor, so he can tryst the night away with his muse."

"But they're really kind of pathetic, aren't they?" Rox asked.

"What do you mean?" I countered. "I've been talking about how pathetic *I* am."

"Oh, you're just feeling sorry for yourself. You'll get over that soon, I know that by now."

"Thanks."

"Don't mention it. Where was I?"

"Phoebe and Steve. Pathetic."

"Right. It *is* pathetic. He's got to see himself as a great artist, and she, apparently has to play these games as a femme fatale, and all the while they're playing these Noel Coward–oh-so-sophisticated open-marriage games." I rubbed my chin. "You have a point, maybe. The thing is, as far as I can tell, Stephen *has* all the attributes of a great artist. Except talent. He's passionately devoted to poetry, knows a lot about it, works hard at it, and doesn't really care about anything else, including his marriage. Then he sits down and sweats and pours out his heart and writes *is this a head?*"

"Phoebe's probably pretty successful attracting other guys," Rox said. "A lot of men are attracted to that fragile, seemingly helpless type. Women like that help them assuage their macho bruises in the wake of feminism."

"Is this how you talk to your professors?"

"Sort of," she said. "I have to make what I'm saying more obscure. You're not having any trouble following me, I trust?"

"Lead on."

She smiled. "Good. Attend, then. First I want to say that I love you for scorning Phoebe. Second, I want to get back to the point. The real pathetic thing about the whole business is that while the two of them are out there pretending, posing, and being the biggest pseuds imaginable, they sit inches from all the *real* power, influence, and importance anybody could imagine. They don't even have to ask for it—it's all there waiting in trust for Stephen. All he's got to do is take it."

"How do you know all this?"

"Idle chat during tea. My Network stock is set up the same way. I get the dough from it, but I don't vote it until I tell the lawyers I want to."

"So that's what Lady Arking was talking about on Monday night, saying Stephen might want to fire her."

"Exactly. And of course, Stephen wants no part of it. You can *fail* running a business."

"Whereas," I said, "you can't really fail as a poet, because nobody reads it anyway."

I reached for another scone, doctored it up, and took a bite. I corralled a little blob of cream with my tongue, and said, "You can, however, fail as a detective, and that I have been doing on this case."

"You're under no obligation—" she began.

"I know, I know. But it bothers me. I used to be good at this. I didn't like doing it especially, but I was good at it."

Roxanne said, "Mmmmm. So what are you going to do now, my love?"

"I," I said, "am going to follow Cobb's Principle. Not much else I can do."

"Cobb's Principle? What's that?"

"Surely I must have enunciated it for you at some time or other."

She batted her eyelashes at me. "You've enunciated so many."

I thought she was going to add, "and don't call me Shirley," but she skipped it. She has a lot of self-control, that woman.

"Cobb's Principle," I enunciated, "states that when it is impossible to think of something intelligent to do, one should do something stupid."

"Oh," she said. "That one."

"Yeah, that one. What's the matter?"

"How come with you 'stupid' always has to mean 'dangerous'?"

Depends what you mean by dangerous, I suppose. I went walking the streets of a ghetto bouncing a basketball. It was the way I spent most of my teenage years. I wanted to be the best; Harlem was where the best games were. I had to go there to find them.

One of the greatest compliments of my life was delivered by Sonny Boy Jeffries, who probably described himself on his income-tax forms as a "freelance pharmaceuticals distributor."

Sonny Boy had apparently once cherished NBA dreams before he found an even more lucrative field. He used to park his custom-built black-and-gold Cadillac near the playground. One time after a particularly tight game, he called me over.

I went. Even a white boy knew that when Sonny Boy Jeffries called you, you went. I went, but I didn't like it. Sonny Boy was perfectly capable of telling me to get my white ass out of there and never be seen north of 110th again, or of wasting me on the spot.

Instead, he grinned big under the perpetual dark glasses, and said, "Boy, you done played yourself *black* as far as I'm concerned. Anybody give you any trouble about playin' up here, you tell them to take it up with Sonny Boy."

The amazing thing was, I never had to. Armored with that endorsement, I traveled with confidence, and was never hassled beyond anything I couldn't handle personally.

Sonny Boy is doing life in Attica, at the moment, a fate I wish on all freelance pharmaceutical distributors without exception. But I do have a tiny soft spot for Sonny Boy for seeing past my skin to what I had inside. A lot of more respectable people just can't do that.

I was walking through the black neighborhoods of South East London. The idea was to try to plug in with the neighbors, acquaintances, and friends, if any, of the late, and so far as I know, unlamented, Winston Blake.

Why? Got me. I guess I had some sort of feeling that Winston was too much a cipher—*insert juvie delink hitman here*—and like Aliou and Weiskopf as well, who were dead before I ever got to know them.

I'd read everything Bristow had found out about Winston, which wasn't much. But there was one thing—he'd apparently been a bit of a basketball player. Not that you could blame the guy. Once you spoke to his mother ("He was a good boy, at heart, I don't know what went wrong," unquote) and a few of the guys he'd been arrested with in his abbreviated day ("I don't know nuffink, Copper"), and sent a few detectives to talk to snitches and the neighborhood in general (nobody knew nuffink), what do you do?

You go to a sporting goods store, buy a rubber playground basketball, get into your sweats, and walk around Winston's turf doing some fancy dribbles along the sidewalk, trying to take the newness off it.

*Killed in the Fog* **165**

I ran into another, unexpected problem. Another part of the difficulties I had with playing this game, so to speak, on the road.

I couldn't find a basketball court.

I'd never expected the place to be like New York, where every paved lot that isn't being built on at the moment has hoops at either end (some of the few things about New York's outdoor physical plant that are almost never vandalized, by the way). Nor did I expect Suburbia, USA, with a garage behind every house, and a hoop over every garage.

I did, however, expect *something,* if only because you couldn't go past ten billboards in London that fall without seeing Charles Barkley selling sneakers, or Shaquille O'Neal selling tickets for an NBA exhibition game at Wembley Arena.

My mistake. After about two hours of wandering, I'd drawn some curious looks but no place to play. The only outdoor basketball court I knew of in London was still the one back in Hammersmith, just on the north side of the bridge, just a couple of blocks from TVStrato headquarters, a place I regretted ever setting foot inside.

I finally found one, on a mostly deserted block, locked in behind a cyclone fence. There was one encouraging sign—the corner of the gate had been bent back, making a triangle of space big enough for somebody determined to fit through, even if he was six foot two and weighed a hundred ninety-five pounds. By basketball standards, I'm stocky.

So now, here I was, on a b-ball court at last. There was a discouraging sign, too. It was possible that the fence had been vandalized not to gain access to the court to play on it, but to vandalize it too. The left-hand basket had been bent way down out of the horizontal.

The other one was okay, though. You could even, faintly, see the paint lines on the concrete for the foul line and the strange conical foul lane they used for the International Basketball rules that they played in the Olympics and all the European leagues.

And I was alone.

A voice seemed to come to me. *If you bounce it,* it said, *they will come.*

Besides, I'd known it was a stupid idea to start with. It was about one o'clock. In this northern latitude—much farther north than New York—I had about three more hours of operational daylight. At least I could shoot some hoops. It had been a long time.

So I started. I dribbled and shot, dribbled, spun, and shot. I didn't get to do the thing in basketball I did absolutely the best, which was pass, for obvious reasons.

I also didn't get to do any rebounds, for the simple reason that I just couldn't miss. I was in the zone. Me, the ball, and that basket were a closed system, and all of them responded to my will in equal measure. It happens, once in a while, to anyone who devotes a certain amount of effort to a particular game. The great ones spend their careers there.

The rest of us, of course, would love to save it for the Masters, or the Super Bowl, or the NBA finals, but believe me, it's a thrill whenever it happens.

I was so into myself, to the drum solo of my dribbling on the tarmac, to the slap of my sneakers and the thunk of the ball through the netless metal hoop as they combined for a little unrepeatable jazz solo of my very own, it probably took me ten minutes to know I had an audience.

Six kids, various shades, togged out in what looked suspiciously like American sports kit, were gazing at me with wide eyes and serious faces pressed against the fence.

The oldest was about thirteen. They were a little younger than the crowd I had hoped to attract, but, as I was getting tired of reminding myself, this was not New York.

What the hell, I thought, you go with what you've got.

The front of the bent-down rim was about five inches below

where it should have been, or about nine feet, seven inches from the pavement.

That *ought* be enough.

I took one last jumper at the good hoop, pulled it down as it went through as if it were a rebound, and headed off down the court. Just past the foul line, I pulled the ball up and jigged it a little to the left as if I were going to pass it off, which in real life I had done probably seventeen thousand times.

Since there was nobody to pass to, however, I kept it and jumped for the hoop, a white Julius Erving.

And I did it. I threw that ball down the hole like the winner of the slam-dunk competition, something I was never quite able to do with a legitimate basket.

It felt *good,* even if it was cheating.

That brought some applause from the peanut gallery.

That was what I'd been hoping for. I stood facing them, with the ball against my hip, catching my breath and smiling. I waved to them.

"Come on in," I said.

As soon as they believed I meant it (and as if I had any right to be inviting people in or keeping them out in the first place), they came on in through the fence and joined me on the court.

Any group of kids like this tends to throw up a spokesman. In this case, it wasn't the biggest kid, or the oldest kid—it was a suspicious-eyed youngster of about eleven.

"You're from America, then," he told me.

"Yeah," I said. "You knew that from just three words?"

"Words? No, nothing like words."

I looked down at myself. My whole outfit had been purchased in England. Roxanne and I had left New York in such a rush that I packed in the unconscious assumption that I still had a job. I brought a wardrobe with me that could handle any business demand, but which was painfully deficient when it came to dressing for leisure time, which I now had nothing but.

So he didn't tell I was an American by the clothes I was wearing.

"The way you done that last shot. The way you play in general, ain't it?" The kid explained. "Nobody around here can do that sort of thing. That's NBA-level stuff, that is."

"Not quite," I said.

"Who are you?" the kid demanded.

I switched hands with the basketball and stowed it on my left hip to be free to shake hands.

"Matt Cobb," I said. "Who are you?"

I collected a bunch of names and handshakes. The spokesman's name was Philip.

"Don't mean that," Philip informed me. "What team are you with? What are you doing here? This is one of those charity fings, innit?"

"I thought he was Michael Jordan," came another voice.

"Don't be daft," said the biggest kid. "Michael Jordan is black."

"And about a thousand times better," I said.

"Look pretty good to us," Philip said.

"Thanks. I played in university."

The big kid's name was Thomas. He wore a Chicago Bulls jacket. Bulls gear was pretty common around London, probably because it looks tough and flashy in black and red, and the bull logo is neat.

But Thomas seemed to wear the thing as if he meant it, as if he'd a glimpse of something he might really like and wanted a way to get more.

"Show us some more stuff, then," he said.

I shook my head. The boys looked disappointed but resigned, as though life had accustomed them to disappointment.

"I'm not in show business," I said. "I just want to play some hoops. You up for that?"

"I'm on your side," Philip said.

I laughed. "I think I'd better coach and ref," I said.

The afternoon turned into a clinic. Basic skills, dribbling, passing, free throws. And shooting baskets, of course. Until you get a very sophisticated view of the game, scoring is where all the joy of it comes from.

They were all rank beginners, of course. Until recently, if you can believe this, the view in England of basketball was of a boring game for wimps—the way Americans feel about soccer. Maybe the way most of them have seen it played, it is.

Still, Thomas showed some definite promise. He was the first to catch on that you had to trust the laws of physics to bring the ball back up to your hand when you dribbled it, because if you looked at the ball, you weren't watching your teammates, the basket, or the enemy.

He had a pretty good eye for the hoop, too.

After a while, I let the other kids play some chaotic two-on-two under the one good basket and took Thomas aside.

"You've played this game before, haven't you?"

He took it, as intended, for praise, and grinned. "Couple of times. They used to have a program at the yoof center, but they got their budget cut before I was really old enough to be in it. Me mum doesn't like me out after dark."

"Smart mum," I said. "Listen," I went on, "did you ever hear of a guy named Winston Blake? I understand he played a little basketball in the neighborhood."

"What, Winston? Yeah, older guy. Spent a couple years in Canada, picked up the game there, he said. Seen him play a couple of times. Best around here. Not a shade on you, though."

"Seen him around lately?"

"Seen who?"

It was Philip, the brains of the outfit, who with some street-kid radar had worked out what was going on. The streets, for better or worse, always have a code, and there's always somebody like Philip around to make sure it gets enforced.

This was going to be a little harder than I'd hoped. Nothing to do for it but to meet the challenge head on.

"Winston Blake," I said. "Light-skinned black, early twenties, a little shorter than me."

Thomas said, "He's dead," at the same time Philip said, "We don't know nothing."

"I know he's dead. I want to know what he was up to just before."

"You a copper?"

"I'm an American, for God's sake."

Philip wasn't being fobbed off with that. "There's American coppers," he said.

I dropped my voice real low and terse. "All right. You're a smart lad. You've figured it out that far, let's see if you can take it the rest of the way."

He was suspicious. "What's that mean?"

"You know what happened to Winston?"

Thomas knew that one. "He done some African, then got topped himself." He was so proud to know the answer, he went on with the business right through Philip's vigorous shushing.

"Right," I said. "Now. Put it together. Englishman who's spent time in Canada wastes an African in London, and is done himself by person or persons unknown. Here's your question. I can't possibly give you any help with the answer. What kind of Yank comes around a place like this asking questions about him?"

Philip was impressed in spite of himself. "See Eye Ay?" he whispered.

I pursed my lips. "I thought you were clever lads," I said. "For the record of course, you're absolutely wrong; I'm just a meddling busybody who doesn't know when I'm well out of things. Right?"

They both swore they believed me, which made sense in a way, because I was telling a desperately uncomfortable truth.

"So," I said. "Humor the foreigner. Did you see or here anything of or about Winston before he wasted the African?"

"Do meddling busybodies have a reward budget, then?" Philip asked.

"They might. What do you know?"

Unlike a lot of more experienced snitches, Philip was at least realistic.

"Not a lot, actually. He was around the neighborhood the Friday before, you know, at the Dog & Breakfast, making loud noises about this big 'job' he'd got on, and how the fringe benefits were delightful. He didn't half think *he* was the clever lad."

"Idiots usually do."

"What do you mean?" Philip asked. "He was on for five thousand quid."

"He *thought* he was on for five thousand quid. He was really on for three lead pills, wasn't he?"

"Ya, right," Philip said. Thomas tilted his head and looked intelligent, as if he were beginning to evolve the maxim "Crime Does Not Pay" from first principles.

"In fact," I went on, "if he were ever in line for the five grand at all, which I doubt, going around and shooting his mouth off about it was the very best way to turn gold to lead."

"Ya, right," Philip said again. "He *was* an idiot, wasn't he?"

"Absolutely. What kind of fringe benefit was he talking about?"

"I don't even know what that *is*," Thomas said.

"It's like the guy who delivers the crisps gets to use the van for the family on the weekend," Philip explained.

"Exactly," I said. "Didn't he mention anything specific like that?"

"Wait a minute," Philip said. "If Winston was an idiot for talking, how come I'm not one for talking to you?"

I smiled. "Because I'm the good guys," I said.

Philip still looked skeptical; Thomas, as usual, followed his lead.

There was a zip-up pocket in the back of my sweats. I pulled a nylon wallet out of there, extracted a couple of tens, and handed one each to Thomas and Philip.

"And then, there's that," I said. I gestured with my head back over to where the three younger kids were still having fun with the ball. "See that they get a piece of that, okay?"

"You may want your money back," Philip said, and Thomas looked pained.

"Why?"

"Because Winston never said nuffink about what his fringe benefit was. All he said was what I've already told you."

"Don't worry about it," I said.

I had no complaints. Thanks to the kids, I had places to go and questions to ask. I could keep the investigation going, and a lot of times that's the most you can ask.

And I'd already learned a couple of concrete things. Winston might have been a hood, but as a professional hit man he was a good English basketball player.

Pros don't talk. Period.

Pros don't usually wind up ventilated by the people who've hired them, either.

This led me to conclude that the person who'd hired and killed Winston Blake was no criminal mastermind, either. It was a start.

My reflections were interrupted by Philip's asking me what I was going to do now.

"Why?"

"Because it's getting dark, and it's not too safe for white folks around here after dark."

I looked at the sky and thought, He's right. Half a lifetime and more since Sonny Boy Jeffries had called me over to his car and I was afraid again.

I called to one of the little kids to throw me the ball. I caught it, bounced it once, then put up a long hook shot from where I stood. It swished through. I still couldn't miss.

"Keep the ball, guys," I told them. "Practice what I showed you. I'll be back." In the daytime, I thought.

I was sad and vaguely ashamed as I left.

## 18

**"Let the entertainment begin!"**

Jennifer Saunders
*French & Saunders*, BBC

*A*nd the next night, I was standing in front of a mirror trying to get my black tie just right for another foray back into Christieland.

"Why don't you wear a clip-on like everybody else?" Rox asked.

"Because you can't get them big enough," I said. "Especially nowadays, with these wimpy little Pee Wee Herman ties fashionable with tuxes. I refuse to wear a bow tie that's not as big across as my lips."

"You could pucker up all the time," she suggested.

"You pucker up," I told her.

She did, I took advantage of it, then went back to my tie.

Rox was all ready to go. She had on a backless, strapless number once again, this time in a shimmering purple. I didn't know where it came from, but then I didn't know where the silver one she'd fetched me from prison in on Monday had come from either. One of Roxanne's many extraordinary—I'm tempted to say supernatural—excellences is that she never seems to shop. Things she needs just seem to turn up, without any wear and tear on shoe leather.

Even better, she spares me the classic woman's gambit "How does this look?" Every other woman I've ever known has pulled this one. You know how it goes. She asks how it looks. If you tell her it looks great, she then takes the next ten minutes telling you how it makes her look fat, and her legs look short, and the color makes her eyes look like mud.

So the next time, you look long and hard, and tell her that maybe the dress makes her world-renowned slim, gorgeous hips look perhaps maybe a bit deceptively more voluptuous than the reality with which you are delightfully acquainted might reflect.

The response to this is, "If you mean I'm *fat,* just say so!" followed by tears, the cancellation of the social engagement for which the dress is to be bought, followed by two weeks of a diet of steamed lettuce.

I have decided that the only safe response for the man to make is to fake a heart attack the second he hears the question.

Fortunately, as long as I stay with Ms. Schick, I'll never have to do that. She shows up looking gorgeous, I tell her so, and she believes me.

"Matt Cobb," she said, "fashion prima donna," she said. "You want to make the ambassador wait?"

That was the excuse for all of tonight's gorgeosity. Lady Arking was adding ten more channels to TVStrato's, two of which were U.S. cable networks, and a third of which relied heavily on U.S. programming.

The U.S. ambassador had agreed to attend. This was to accomplish a couple of things. The drawback to being an ambassador is that you can never go to a person's party because you happen to know there will be good hors d'oeuvres. Every move you make sends a message.

The new administration, in the person of Jake Grevey, the tire magnate who was the new ambassador, was sending two messages:

1. America likes to have foreigners pay for things we make, even if they're only old TV shows and

2. Screw the French.

France's paranoia about American cultural products had been the talk of Europe lately. French ministers had been saying things like, "If zis is allowed to continue, directors like Jean-Luc Godard will starve because of the latest sequel to *Jurassic Park*."

Not only that, but they say it as if it were a *bad* thing. I've seen a whole lot of French movies, and if you ask me, the only good thing about World War II is that it kept down the number of them in existence.

Anyway, the French were incredibly cheesed off at American culture for making them long for exotic things like dinosaur movies and actual toilet bowls in restaurants instead of holes in the floor. They were also extremely peeved at Lady Arking and TVStrato for dropping it all over Western Europe from the sky.

Now, why, you may wonder, wouldn't the French simply ban the reception of TVStrato, thereby keeping the nation safe for boring, pseudointellectual, pretentious, bullshit movies that nobody except a French intellectual would ever want to see?

Because they can't. Because the European Union, formerly the European Community, formerly the Common Market, has a treaty stating that if one member country deems a program or service fit for satellite broadcast, no other country can keep it out.

So Lady Arking was adding channels—American cartoons and American sports, plus a general channel with plenty of off-Network series, and the American ambassador was going to be there to celebrate.

The French ambassador had sent his regrets.

Roxanne and I were last-minute additions to the guest list. The party had been in the works for months, one of the reasons this current unpleasantness hadn't led to its cancellation.

The other reason, quite frankly, was that none of the current unpleasantness had yet managed to attach itself to Lady Arking in the public prints.

The party remained on, and Rox and I were going. We had been asked for, we had been assured, by the ambassador himself.

We speculated on this.

"He probably wants to know," Rox said, "why you happen to be around when so many English people get bumped off."

"Only *two*," I protested. "*I* think he saw you on Monday's news, and wants to see you in an evening gown again. I know I'm enjoying it."

"I'm glad," she said. "You know, you look pretty scrumptious in formal attire yourself. We should do this more often. If you can learn how to tie your tie."

"I think I've almost—"

"Oh, give me that," she said.

She advanced on me with her hands out and grabbed my neck as if she planned to strangle me.

When she pulled away, the tie was perfect.

"How did you do that?"

"Putting bows in dolly hair. Now don't touch it."

"Yes, ma'am."

I walked to the front room, hooked the curtain aside, and looked out the window. The limousine was just pulling up outside the house.

"He just got here," I told Rox. "All that impatience, and I wasn't even late."

I helped her on with her coat. It was fuzzy, but not fur. She's not militant about it, she just prefers not to wear it.

Whatever it was, it was warm enough. Considering that it was the only thing between her and a very cold, very damp November night, Rox showed nary a shiver as we approached the open door of the car.

I recognized our old friend Nigel, also known as James, holding the door.

"Sorry about the lack of excitement," I told him. "No photographers."

He touched the brim of his cap.

"That's quite all right, sir. I expect all the excitement I can handle from the weather tonight."

"How's that?"

"Fog, sir. Not so bad yet, but it's rolling right up the river. The garage was quite socked in with it."

And as if he'd conjured them with his words, white tendrils began creeping along the ground toward us, like tentacles out to grab our legs and pull us away with them somewhere.

It was spooky. I jumped inside the car and let James close the door. I fancied that a bit of tendril was clipped off inside the Jag with us, but it soon dissipated and died.

"There's no rush," Roxanne assured Nigel when he took his own seat. "Be careful."

Under her breath she muttered, "And if the ambassador has to wait, he'll just have to lump it."

It was weird outside. In New York, usually, you wake up in the morning, look out the window, and see what looks like the inside of a cotton ball. Or you walk out of a theater into a world where a taxicab couldn't see you even if it wanted to stop for you. The little cat feet stuff was strictly poetry.

This was the first time I'd ever seen fog actually moving in and occupying territory, and it was a weird experience. It resembled some kind of creature, but cat wasn't even in the running. My personal money would be on something out of the Cthulu Mythos.

Then I thought of something else, and put a much brighter face on things. "Hey," I said. "This is it. This is the first. Three months and change, and we've finally seen one."

"Seen one what?" Rox demanded.

*Killed in the Fog*   **179**

"The famous London fog. Fabled in song and story and five thousand black-and-white cop movies with William Hartnell that Channel Eleven in New York used to show at three o'clock in the morning when I was a kid."

"Who was William Hartnell?" Rox wondered.

"Rox, I'm hurt. Are you hurt, Nigel?"

"I'm not allowed to have emotions when I'm driving, sir."

"Oh," I said, "very sensible. If you *were* allowed to have emotions, would you be hurt?"

"Absolutely bleeding, sir."

"Thank you," I said. I turned to Rox. "See? As soon as Nigel gets off duty and can have emotions again, he's going to bleed."

"Cobb," Rox informed me flatly, "life with you is a nonstop laugh riot. So who was he, already?"

"Precisely."

Then, before we wandered too far into an Abbott and Costello routine, I told her. "In addition to playing army sergeants and cops, William Hartnell was the first Doctor Who."

"Oh. I like the blond one."

I turned my attention back to the fog. The limo was so vibration free that it was only the stray lamppost looming out of the whiteness or the occasional set of yellow lights, visible as a soft glow, that gave us any feeling of motion at all.

I looked around and said, "Nigel, maybe we ought to give this up."

His voice showed no panic, but no pleasure, either. "I've considered it, sir, but I really think it would be worse to go back than to press on."

"Really?"

"Yes, sir. We're more than halfway there."

I shrugged. The man was a professional, after all. It wasn't as if we were on a superhighway, where the smashup of one vehicle was a potential hundred-car catastrophe. And it wasn't like a blizzard, where visibility and traction disappeared simultaneously.

"Press on, then," I told him.

"With the utmost care, sir."

"Great."

"Used to get fogs like this quite frequently when I was a lad. All the coal that used to be burnt. Hardly ever see them, anymore. They used to last for days."

I was just as glad they didn't last for days anymore. I didn't like this. This fog was more conducive to claustrophobia than a locked phone booth. It was like being inside a big white balloon that rolled with you every time you took a step, so you could never get out, or even approach the skin.

When we entered the park, things were a little better. We could measure our progress by the quaint little lamps alongside the road. Jillionaires' row, along the canal, was also well lit, mostly with security-inspired floodlights. Even if you couldn't see the individual houses too well, you could make out where they were in the midst of the icy sculptures of fog and ice that surrounded them.

I'd done some boning up on this particular development since we'd been here last. People had to pay *£600,000 a year* just for the lot. Houses were built at the owner's own expense. With that kind of money tied up in a place to live, I'd have floodlights, too.

"We're getting close," I said.

"How can you tell?" Roxanne asked.

"Lady Arking's place is the last one in the row, down near the zoo. Listen."

I rolled down the window a little more so she could hear. The world gets quiet in a fog, and sounds carry. Rox could hear the grunts, wails, and howls from the zoo. The animals didn't like the fog, either.

I gave her my best Bela. "Leezen to dem," I said. "Cheeldren off de night—vat music *dey* make."

"You're sick," she said.

Nigel pulled the car up a gravel drive. If I were paying almost a million dollars a year just to rent the land my house stood on, I personally would have a paved driveway, but there's probably some kind of class thing about it that I haven't caught on to yet.

One of the nice things about being an American in England is that you're outside the class system. More important, it's outside of you. You don't have to be intimidated by anybody, and better yet, there are no constraints of custom and convention to keep you from being friends with anybody you please.

For example, I could spend part of the trip engaged with friendly banter on an equal basis with Nigel. For all he kept calling me "sir," he was giving nothing away in that talk, and we both had fun.

Stephen Arking, for instance, could never have that sort of conversation with someone who, I suppose, he would call a servant, and not just because Stephen was a jerk, either. Bernard Levering couldn't have done it, and he's not only "middle class," he's had the advantage of a sojourn in the States to insulate him from all the bullshit.

Banbridge let us in and took Roxanne's coat. There was appreciation in his elderly eyes as she was revealed. She saw it and smiled at him. Class system or no class system, butlers don't smile back, but it was easy to see that he was pleased.

We were led by a subordinate (Banbridge had to stay and receive guests, after all) into a place we hadn't been before. Hadn't even expected it, though I suppose I should have in a place that big.

It was a room draped with blue satin, big enough to hold at least three basketball courts the size of the one I'd met the kids on the day before yesterday.

There was a band on a raised platform at the far end of the room. The place in between was dotted with people dancing and glittering.

James Bond, of course, could have walked into that situation and owned it. I was not James Bond. I was, all of a sudden, little

Matty Cobb from Manhattan, sneaking in with the grown-ups. It was as if the class system was serving notice that I hadn't escaped it as easily as I thought.

Then I remembered Carol Burnett's trick for not being nervous at auditions—picture the person auditioning you on the toilet.

I didn't go so far as to picture a hundred rich people sitting on commodes (each of which would undoubtedly flush in a different way), but I did get a laugh out of it, and that broke the spell.

"Thank you," I whispered to Roxanne.

"What for?" she whispered back.

"For not living in this world," I said. "For not making me live in it."

"What do you think I was running away from?"

"More than this," I said.

"Sure, but this was a big part of it. Be ready to make nice."

I said, "Huh?" and looked around; it took me a second or two to realize what she was talking about.

There hadn't been a trumpet fanfare or a stentorian announcement of who we were when we entered (not that I would have put it past whoever was organizing the party), but through some arcane ballroom telegraph, our Presence Was Known, and Lady Arking was bearing down on us with hostessy good wishes.

"How do you do," she said to both of us. "I am truly glad you could come. The ambassador will be so delighted when he gets here."

"I'm glad we haven't upstaged him."

"No, he's been delayed by the fog. It's quite inconvenient."

I reflected that her ladyship, slowly but surely, was regaining her imperious style, despite the fact that the Aliou mess remained as messy as ever. She was dressed in her trademark bright red, this time in an evening gown of shimmering satin, like Roxanne's purple number. But where the shimmering fabric on Rox suggested a gift wrap concealing something wonderful, on Lady Arking it looked like armor.

Off in the distance, Phoebe, in some fluffy orange thing, gave me a playful wave. I ignored it.

"I'll introduce you to him as soon as he arrives," Lady Arking said, and smiled a combined blessing and dismissal.

I left Rox to mingle, and went to see if I could find us something nonalcoholic to drink, by no means a sure thing at any English gathering. I was making good progress across the dance floor, since the fog had held down the crowd, when I ran into Bernard Levering.

In my current mood, it was nice to see a familiar face. I greeted him like a brother. "Bernard!" I said.

"Cobb, you bastard," he sneered. "I ought to smash your bloody face."

# 19

*I* looked at him.

"You," I said, "are the last thing I need. What's eating you, anyway?"

"As if you didn't know."

"God, I hate that. Look. You tell me what you think the problem is. If you think I already know it, add hypocrisy to the list of complaints."

Bernard looked puzzled.

"How drunk are you?" I asked.

"Hah!" he said. "I am *totally* drunk. I am blind pissed drunk. I find it hard to believe I am able to stand up and articulate."

"If that's the case," I said, "how do you propose to smash my bloody face in?"

He mulled that one over.

"It might present a bit of difficulty," he allowed, "but I mean to have a bloody good try!"

I managed to catch his fist before he got it up too high, and convince him to relax it without doing anything drastic—i.e., hitting him, hurting him, or knocking him off his drunken balance. Anybody seeing us probably thought we were exchanging a club handshake.

My restraint seemed to infuriate him all the more.

"Bastard," he hissed. "I ought to—"

I tightened my grip on his wrist a little. He winced. "You ought to control yourself. Listen, Bernard, I don't know Lady Arking as well as you do, but somehow I doubt she'd appreciate a brawl during this occasion."

"Stuff her. And stuff you, too."

"Unlikely, in either case. Suppose we find a seat, and you can tell me what I did, okay? If we stand here holding hands like this, people are going to get ideas. We might even wind up with our own sitcom on Channel Four."

Bernard liked that one. It made it possible for me to lead him away.

"One thing about you, Cobb. You've got a great sense of humor. You're a bastard, but you've got a great sense of humor."

"I sure do," I said ruefully, and that was so funny, he had to be off laughing again.

Actually, I did better than find a seat. I found his wife. And my fiancée at the same time. They were seated at a table picking out some hors d'oeuvres from a silver tray proffered by a uniformed waiter. The waiter was good. His face and body language said that it was his greatest pleasure on earth to stand there until the next ice age, if necessary, waiting for the ladies to make up their minds.

I got Bernard to the table, and he joined the fun, though I admit he made up his mind a lot faster than the women did. It was good that he eat something, anyway. It would slow down the absorption of any alcohol remaining in his stomach, assuming his bloodstream could hold any more.

He ate very fastidiously. While he did so, I said hello to the ladies. Sandy kissed me on the cheek, and we picked a few snacks ourselves, and the waiter stifled a scream of relief as he was finally allowed to straighten his back.

I had always liked Sandy. She was a looker in the big-featured, big-boned way of the pre-anorexia Carly Simon. A definite New York type, with the no b.s. attitude and the quick wit that went with her looks.

"Okay, Matt," she said, "what have you done to him?"

"Oh, don't *you* start. He came up to me and said he ought to smash my bloody face in."

"Omigod," Sandy said. "He didn't try to do it, did he?"

I told her the attempt had been nipped in the bud with no harm done to anybody's person or reputation.

"The trouble is," I went on, "that I can't get him to tell me why he thinks he ought to be mad at me."

"Really, Matt, we've always been friends, but can you honestly blame him?"

"Cut it *out!* I don't know what I can blame and not blame. All I know is that an old friend of mine is *very* drunk, and he offered to rearrange my face at the risk of job and possible arrest."

"Arrest?" Roxanne asked. "Matt, he didn't even hit you."

"I said at the risk of. I say nothing of the risk of my knocking his block off, but I have been in a bad mood lately and I almost swung first and asked questions later. You hear me, Bernard?"

Almost certainly, Bernard did not. He had his elbows on the table and his chin in his hands. He was staring straight ahead with a fixed grin on his kisser, and little buzzing snores escaped from the corners of his mouth.

His wife appraised him.

"This is good. This is the final stage. If everybody leaves him alone, he'll sleep just like that for forty-five minutes. When he wakes up, his forearms will be numb, and he'll have a killer headache, but he'll be sober. Trust my Bernard to figure out a way to have the morning after on the same night."

"Fine," I said. "I'll be back in forty-five minutes to ask him what his problem is. Want to dance, Rox?"

This was a crock, and she knew it. I do not dance. Still, she said sure, and rose to come with me.

Rox was in the middle of telling Sandy what a pleasure it had been to meet her when Sandy said, "Matt. Roxanne. Wait, please."

We sat.

Sandy looked hard at me.

"You really didn't know what's going on?"

I made a frustrated noise in my throat. "What is it, something in the air in this country? How many times do I have to say something before anybody believes I'm really saying it?"

Sandy put her hand on mine, just for a second.

"Matt, I'm sorry. And when Sleeping Beauty over there wakes up, he'll be sorry, too. The thing is, if you don't know what's going on, I *really* don't know what's going on. What the hell is she up to?"

I thought I caught the drift. "By 'she,' I assume you mean Phoebe?"

Sandy was more baffled than ever. "Phoebe? What could that washed-out little shrimp have to do with anything?"

"Yeah," I said. If she only knew. "I guess I was just being silly."

"It's not Phoebe. It's the Queen Bee. The Boss. Lady Arking."

"What is *she* doing? That concerns me, I mean."

"Matt, she's organizing this big purge at TVStrato. She's ordered Bernard to get together confidential dossiers on all the employees. She says there are terrible security leaks in the organization, and she's going to get rid of them if she has to fire the lot."

"When was this?"

"This afternoon."

"Ah," I said. Apparently, I'd been wrong about Lady Arking beginning to put the whole unfortunate business behind her. What she'd actually done was put it all in front of her, so she could fight it the better. No wonder she'd picked a dress that sat on her like iron.

It occurred to me that she would have been most happy tonight armed with a Winchester repeater (to pick off renegades from horseback), and dressed in an Annie Oakley outfit of buckskin skirt and blouse, both complete with fringe.

"So she's in heavy paranoia mode. I got the impression when I talked to Bernard that fateful day that she frequently is."

"Not as badly as this," Sandy said. "And when Bernard objected to spying on his fellow employees that way, she threatened to get rid of him, as well."

"She couldn't do it," I said. "She couldn't run the place without him."

Sandy tightened her lips.

"She thinks she can. Especially since she told Bernard in so many words that you were being brought in to run the screening. And, she implied, anything else you wanted to run. The bitch."

"She said that, huh?"

"See?" Sandy said. "Now you don't believe *me*."

"I believe you, I believe you. It's her ladyship I don't believe. Tell her, Rox."

"Well, she did offer him a job—to set up a Special Projects department for TVStrato—"

Sandy said, "Yeees?" She sounded like the Great Gildersleeve.

"—But Matt turned her down. Cold. Said he'd only look into aspects of it that were outside the business, and he was only doing that much because we'd become unintentionally involved in the case."

I noticed Rox's use of the word "we" and appreciated it. She hadn't wanted anything to do with it.

"Okay," Sandy said. "I'm just talking hypothetically here, all right? I mean I know you live together, but you're not Siamese twins. Maybe Matt has made a deal with the old lady and hasn't gotten around to telling you yet?"

"Why would he do that?" Roxanne demanded. "Not only are we engaged to be married . . ."

Sandy's face lit up in a wide, unfeigned grin.

"You *are?* She practically squeaked it. *"Mazel tov!"*

I love New Yorkers.

Sandy asked when the happy day was; Rox said we were still working on it, which was a pretty tactful way of putting it.

"And even if we weren't involved with each other, I'm the principal stockholder in the Network; Matt's a vice-president. I'm not active in running the Network, but if a VP leaves to take another job somewhere, Tom Falzet tells me, if only to be polite. How long could Matt keep it from me? What good would it be doing him if he did?"

Sandy shrugged sheepishly. "It was only a hypothesis. *A* hypothesis? I was never any good at that. Are you trying to tell me, Rox, that if he did that he would lose you?"

"No," she said. "I'm telling you that if he were the kind of person who would do that, he never would have had me in the first place."

Sandy nodded wisely. "You'd have to be an idiot to give up that kind of fringe benefit."

There was that word again. Maybe I was trying to tell me something. I sort of tuned out of the conversation and explored the idea. There were some interesting corridors to probe while I was wandering around in the old subconscious. They led from interesting to fascinating, from fascinating to frightening.

This was the way it always was. I was dashing around in my memory and imagination, opening new doors, tracing connections I hadn't suspected before.

Sandy and Rox went on talking; I remember odd flashes of the conversation.

". . . So glad you can finally get Marshmallow Fluff in this country. When you need a Fluffernutter, you just need one. . . ."

". . . Used to be so polite, but nobody queues for buses, anymore. . . ."

". . . My God, look, now the other one's in a trance, too. . . ."

". . . And don't worry, if I know Matt, he'll have a few words to say to Lady Arking when he sees her. . . ."

That last bit broke through.

"Lady Arking!" I said.

"Where?" the two women demanded.

"We've got to find her!"

Sandy asked Roxanne if I was always like this.

"Mostly, he's pretty normal. Sometimes he's worse." Rox turned to me. "Matt," she said, "has something happened?" She sounded just like Cloris Leachman asking Lassie if Jeff was okay. "Something that makes it urgent that we find her right away? Because remember, she'll come looking for us as soon as the ambassador gets here."

"No, nothing's happened, except that a hunch just bit me. Yes, if my hunch is right, we'd better do it right away, and stick with her until I can organize something to wind this thing up.

"Sandy, you can help, too. Can you leave Bernard without his falling over and cracking his head?"

"Sure," she said. "The one thing I regretted about leaving the Network was never having a chance to get in on one of your Special Projects parties."

"Is that what they called them? Parties?"

"Usually. I think Harris Brophy started it."

"Figures. Okay, here's what you do. Circulate. Find the old lady."

"Shouldn't be hard," Sandy said. "She's taller than I am, and she's dressed like a fire engine."

"That's right. So find her and stick to her like a limpet. Then don't let her out of your sight until *I* find her, okay?"

"Sure," she said again. "Bernard is going to be sorry he missed this."

She was off. Roxanne had a strange look on her face, half excitement, half wariness.

"Same instructions for me?" she asked.

"One addition. Before you go looking for Lady Arking, find a phone first. Call Bristow and get him out here."

"In the fog?"

I had forgotten about the fog.

"Yeah," I said. "In the fog. He's got sirens, he won't mind."

"This is it, huh, Cobb?"

"Could be. I hope so. I'm sick of this mess."

"I've known you for a long time, Cobb, but this is only the second one of these things I've been in on the end of. I don't much like it. I'm scared."

I gave her a weak grin.

"Me, too," I said. "Especially about tonight."

"I don't suppose you'd want to give me a little hint of what you're talking about."

"Sure. What is this house full of?"

"Tradition?"

I shook my head. "It seems Victorian, but it's quite new, remember?"

"Food?" Rox asked. "Windows? Guest Rooms? Servants? Guests?"

"You think of them as guests," I said. "Somebody thinks of them as potential suspects."

"Suspects? You mean . . . ?"

"We'll see. Maybe we'll just have a nice session with Bristow and then go home. In the meantime, let's find Lady Arking."

"Right," she said. "Phone first, find Lady Arking."

"Then find me."

"Right."

Roxanne kept saying "right," but she went left, at right angles to Sandy who'd headed straight off across the room. That left the far reaches of the ballroom for me. I decided to got to the far end and work my way back toward the middle.

The crowd, which had looked pretty sparse when we'd first come in, became a teeming multitude when I started trying to sift through it. You'd think it would be easy for a fairly tall man to find a tall woman in a bright red dress no matter how dense the crowd, but you would be wrong.

Of course, it's a lot less easy if the tall woman in the red dress happens not to be there.

That was the conclusion I found myself facing as I swept the floor of the ballroom, looking and looking. I found Sandy twice, and Roxanne once. Sandy had seen Stephen from a distance, she said the second time.

"How about Phoebe?"

"Her, too. She was talking to some guy from Italian television."

"Okay," I said. "The next time you see either one of them, say we're looking for the old lady. Recruit them into the search. It'll be a good idea if they know of our concern."

She wiggled joyfully. "This is really exciting," she said.

"Yeah," I deadpanned, "I'm all aquiver."

Roxanne had spoken to Bristow.

"He didn't like it, but he's coming."

"Good. Keep looking." I told her about the Stephen and Phoebe order.

"Matt?" she said. "Bristow asked me if they should bring guns."

That twisted a short, harsh laugh out of me.

"What did you tell him?"

"I told him you hadn't said anything about it. He said, well, since you seemed to be running things anyway, he wouldn't do it without orders."

"Golly," I said, "what a card."

I gave Rox a quick peck on the cheek and moved off again to mingle.

Some detective. I was beginning to think I couldn't detect my own ass with both hands and a flashlight, when I saw Stephen across the room, guiding along a tall, slim, gray-haired guy. I'd never met Mr. Grevey, and I didn't recall seeing his picture on TV or in the papers, but if the fellow with Stephen wasn't the ambassador, the State Department had missed a bet. I'd never seen anybody who looked so *diplomatic*.

All I had to do now was catch up with them, a task made easier by the fact that they were headed straight for me. The ambassador had a kind of fixed grin on his face. I had a horrible feeling that Stephen was reciting poetry to him.

I caught up with them in the middle of the floor.

The band had been taking a break. Before that, they had been playing soporific stuff one step up from Muzak. Now they had to show their chops, whipping into a high-volume rendition of the old Blood, Sweat & Tears song "Lucretia MacEvil," heavy on the brass. We had to yell to be heard over it.

"Cobb!" Stephen yelled, "Come here!"

He didn't have to ask me twice. I virtually ran, dodging enthusiastic dancers, who had apparently been dying to cut a rug to antique jazz rock for years now.

Now he yelled in Grevey's ear, "Mr. Ambassador, allow me to present your famous countryman Matt Cobb!"

The ambassador gave me a political grin and shook my hand. "I've heard so much about you, Mr. Cobb! It's a pleasure to meet you!"

I said, "Nice to meet you, too!" then abandoned him, thereby blowing any chance I may have ever had for a political career.

"Stephen! Where's your stepmother?"

"What? Pamela has a headache! She frequently gets them! She's gone to lie down!"

"Where's Phoebe?"

"Cobb, Ambassador Grevey has been eager to meet you!"

"I'll explain later!"

"What?"

"I'LL EXPLAIN LATER!!!" I screamed, just as the band stopped. "Where's Phoebe?"

"She went up to give Pamela one of her famous neck rubs. It frequently helps."

I made Stephen tell me how to get to the room, and I ran.

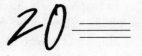

**"And there it is!"**

Tommy Cooper
*The Tommy Cooper Show,* Thames TV

*I* had various pictures in my mind of what I'd find when I made it to the room, depending on when in the proceedings I happened to arrive.

The worst thing to find would be a dead body and nothing else, because nobody was ever going to prove anything in that case. The next worst thing would be to find a dead body and a killer screaming she had just found the body.

The next worst thing, paradoxically enough, would have been to find two completely sound and well women, because then the murderer would draw her horns in and would never be caught.

It would also be awfully embarrassing for me, but I was getting used to that.

The best thing, God help me, was to find a murder attempt *in progress.* That would provide two witnesses (the intended victim and me) and tie up the killer while Bristow and the boys searched for some evidence.

Meanwhile, I kept running. The damned place was bigger than Buckingham Palace. Second flight of stairs, turn right, right again, fifth door on the left.

There it was. The house was too well made for me to have heard any noises through the door, and I didn't want to take the time anyway.

I didn't even try the knob to see if the door was locked. I just backed up against the far wall of the corridor, pushed off as hard as I could, and pistoned my right heel into the door just below the lock.

A cop had shown me how to do that. It doesn't take a lot of strength if you hit in the right place, and I caught it lucky.

The door popped open to rustling noises and darkness. For one horrible moment I was afraid I had blundered in on a couple making love in Lady Arking's bedroom, or that Stephen's directions hadn't been so hot after all.

When the three bullets flashed out of the darkness at me, though (a worst thing I hadn't thought of adding to my list), I decided I must be in the right place after all.

I admire the man or woman who can actually *think* in a situation like that. God knows *I* can't. Sure, in retrospect you can say that if you ducked to the side of the doorway, the killer would still have shot you through the wall, and would have gained time to finish the murder, besides, to say nothing of being able to escape through the window at leisure. At the time though, nothing flashes through your mind except *"hit the floor!"*

So I dived.

*Into* the room.

It really was a brilliant thing to do; I've been congratulating my subconscious ever since. I kicked the door shut behind me as I went down, so now the killer couldn't see me any more than I could see her.

In fact, rolling sideways and ducking two more shots, I could see better, because as my eyes adjusted to the darkness, I could see the top half of her dimly silhouetted against the window, which, curtained as it was, still leaked enough light from the grounds and the park and the zoo to make visible something standing directly in front of it.

I hate guns, and in all the years since I've left the army I've only fired one once. However, every tool finds its time of use, and, boy! could I have used a gun right then. I could have potted the killer virtually at will and the whole business would have been over.

However, as my dear old dad used to say, wish in one hand and shit in the other and see which one gets full first. We would have to do this the hard way.

As soon as I could figure out what that was.

I was on the floor, way over to my left, hugging the dark carpet like a baby chimp clinging to its mother's shoulder. The only movement I had risked was to turn up the collar of my dinner jacket to hide the white of my shirt. Because if my vision was getting better in the darkness, so was the killer's.

I didn't have a lot of time left.

I could see now that between me and my friend with gun was the bed, and on that lay the intended victim, not totally conscious maybe, but, judging from an occasional groan and wiggle, not dead either.

I knew what I was going to do. It might not have been the smartest thing that could have been done in the circumstances, but it was all I could think of, aside from waiting for the gentlemen of the Yard to arrive.

But even that I'd ruined with impatience, turning myself into an instant hostage.

No. I had to get myself and the victim-to-be out of the line of fire, separate the killer from the victim and capture her. That's called strategy.

Tactics were simple. I inched forward—millimetered, actually—on the carpet, trying to make no noise until I was about nine feet, a body length and a half, from the edge of the bed.

Now the idea was to slowly gather my legs under me until I was ready to spring.

No time.

The killer's voice came out of the darkness, more gleeful than I'd ever heard it.

"I see you," she said.

So much for slowly. I jerked like a man with his tongue in a light socket, then scrambled forward under another bullet.

I was leading a charmed life; I didn't want to take any more chances. I crabbed rapidly to the bed, grabbed the bottom of the box spring with both hands, and heaved.

Most English beds are strange by American standards—their box springs are strange, massive, bolted-together affairs that come down to within an inch or so of the floor. There wasn't a lot of room, but I jammed my fingers under as far as they would go, tearing a nail and barking some knuckles in the process. After that, it was just a matter of summoning all my strength. I literally threw the bed with the potential victim on it, in the killer's face.

It worked. Another bullet went into the ceiling as the edge of the bed knocked the killer's arm up. I just stood behind the bed and pushed.

The idea was to get her wedged up against a wall and trapped, but it didn't work. She squirted free and out the French window to the balcony.

I didn't know where she could get to from there, but I'd seen from the drive up that there were stairs down to ground level.

The first thing I had to do was check out the victim. I threw the bed aside and excavated her from tumbled bedclothes.

It was a good thing I did, because a silk scarf was still tight around her throat. If I'd left her, she might just have gone on strangling. I pulled the scarf loose where the ends had been neatly tucked in.

Air sliced into her throat, and she moaned but didn't say anything. A quick feel of the skull showed me the lump. My fingers came away sticky.

Something occurred to me. People being strangled don't moan. Those sounds had to have come from the killer's throat, the killer's twisted emotions. I felt a chill go through me.

"Matt?"

It was Roxanne, along with Stephen Arking and Sandy and Bernard Levering.

I spoke to Stephen. "You got any doctors on the guest list?"

"Yes, but—"

"No buts. Get the doctor. Lady Arking has been hit in the head and choked. She's still alive but she needs medical help. Go."

"But what about Phoebe?" he protested.

"Phoebe's fine for the time being," I told him. "Go get the doctor."

He went.

I turned to Roxanne. "Phoebe's it. Tell Bristow."

Sandy had been right about her husband. He looked like a man with a headache; he looked like man who'd walked in halfway through the movie; but he was not drunk.

"*Phoebe?*" he squeaked. "Little Phoebe?"

"Yeah," I said, "little Phoebe. Sometime when you get the chance count the bullet holes in this room. Not now, though. She's loose, and she's got a gun. I don't care how you do it, but make sure nobody leaves the house. Recruit the servants.

"Also, she may try to get back in. It's a mean night, and I recall she was only wearing this flimsy chiffon thing."

"Organdy," Rox said.

"Thank you," I said. "It was vital that we get that right."

"Ha-ha," she said. "What are you going to do?"

"I'm going to go catch her, if I can." I kissed her quickly and plunged out onto the balcony into the fog.

*William L. DeAndrea* **200**

## 21

**"Safari? So goody!"**

Christopher Biggins
*Biggins' On Safari,* Thames TV

The fog wasn't quite as bad as it had been when we'd first driven up. The night had grown colder; low temperatures were on their way toward turning the fog into a misty rain and precipitating it out of the air.

But that was hours from now.

At the moment, visibility was still limited to a few dozen yards, and the lights shone in a white limbo.

Because of the way the land sloped up away from the canal, it was only one flight of stairs from the balcony to the ground on this side of the house.

At the bottom of the stairs was a small terrace, the gate of which was standing open. Fine, O Mighty Hunter, I thought. Through the gate and after the quarry. Then what?

Then listen. That was what I had going for me in the fog. Most of the world fell silent, and the sounds that *did* occur seemed to travel farther and more clearly.

So I'd rely on sound.

I knew that's what Phoebe would be doing—I had her glasses in my pocket. I had found them just inside the French window. They must have been knocked off when I'd thrown the bed at her. A quick glance through them had shown me that they were very strong glasses, and she probably couldn't see worth a damn without them.

That would probably have made a difference if it weren't for the damned fog.

I closed my eyes, held my breath, and listened hard.

Light, rhythmic clicks. High heels on a paved path. If there were any casual strollers here tonight, I doubted they were wearing heels. I knew there was a gate not far from where I stood that lead out into Regent's Park, through which the canal ran. I stepped to the side of the path—no sense letting her hear me coming—and followed the clicks.

When I got to the gate, it was ajar. Not only that, but a wisp of orange chiffon was snagged on a piece of wire. Organdy.

This was so perfect, I waited a few seconds and thought it over. Suppose, I thought, the hero walks blindly through the fence and catches a couple of bullets out of the fog on the other side. Three of them. Remembering Winston, and her marksmanship through the doorway at me, I knew Phoebe liked to set them off in groups of three.

I let the clicking convince me it was just luck. I went through. Nothing happened. I still kept to the side of the path on the wet grass. The leather soles of my evening shoes slipped occasionally, but that was a small price to pay for stealth. All I had to do was remember not to swear every time it happened.

I wondered why Phoebe hadn't done the same. I knew she couldn't walk on soft ground in spike heels, but she could take them off and walk barefoot on the path. It might not be comfortable, and she did run a risk—London, in my assessment is the dog-poo capital of the world, worse even than New York—but we were playing a high-stakes game here.

And Phoebe had already shown she was a woman who was not averse to taking risks.

Tonight for instance, with the attempt on Lady Arking.

So simple, so opportunistic. Phoebe was good at taking her opportunities where she found them. In this case, it was the well-known fact that Lady Arking got tension headaches, and that Phoebe could give neck rubs that relieved them. So when Lady Arking happened to mention to her stepdaughter-in-law that she could feel one of the damnably inconvenient ones coming on in the middle of her party for the American ambassador (which would never do), all Phoebe had to do was tell her to go lie down in her room for a few minutes until Phoebe had a chance to join her.

That was all she needed by way of an alibi, really. A conk on the head—because after all, Pamela was such a large woman—then one of Lady Arking's own scarves around the neck. A minute or two, to be sure no first aid would be effective, then "discover" the body and scream murder, *à la* Lady Macbeth. Just make sure the gun (she loved guns, did our little Phoebe) was out of your possession and innocent of fingerprints.

Simple. The only real danger is that somebody would blunder in, and that was unlikely. Who could imagine that some wise guy from New York would figure out what the most likely fringe benefit was, put a few things together, and realize what you were up to?

I was making some progress. Either that, or Phoebe was pressing. Either way, the clicks were getting louder.

So were the animal noises. A tree loomed out of the fog—I dodged it just as some bird that was definitely not the nightingale that sang in Berkeley Square let out an unearthly shriek that started a whole jungle cacophony. We were approaching London Zoo.

*Killed in the Fog*  **203**

I've got her, I thought. There was a great big fence around the zoo, all the way around, and the canal ran through the middle of it. Phoebe was going to have to make a huge detour before she got to the main road, and I could sprint along and catch up with her.

Then I heard the gunshot.

I was halfway to the ground before I realized I was being silly. If I couldn't see her through the fog, she sure as hell couldn't see me through the same fog without her glasses.

There was another shot, and the *peeng* of a bullet screaming off metal.

The animals in the zoo went insane.

My God, I thought as I picked myself up from the wet earth, she's picking them off through the fence. I also thought, as I felt the damp seep into my skin, that this tux had about had it.

Then I realized what was really happening. She wasn't going to go around the zoo. She'd shot the lock off the side gate so she could go through.

Again, simple; again, very dangerous. There were guards at the zoo, and a store (as at all zoos) of high-powered rifles to be used in case a dangerous animal got loose.

Then there were the animals. It was a cold night, most of the animals would be safely locked away against the cold night. But not all—witness the sounds. Some animals liked cold. Polar bears for instance.

Only they didn't have polar bears anymore at this zoo. In recent years, they'd devoted themselves exclusively to endangered species and captive breeding programs.

But there was something here, something I'd seen on one of my visits here with Roxanne . . .

I reached the fence. The lock was mangled, and the gate again was ajar. No organdy this time. The path led on through the fog.

I supposed Phoebe's plan was to make her way through the zoo, then shoot the lock off at the other end, hop a cab or a 274 bus to

Baker Street Station, and be off. One problem she might have with the plan was that, by my count, she had already fired eight bullets. Unless she had a store of ammunition and was reloading, the little automatic she was toting around couldn't have more than one bullet left in it, maximum.

I followed her into the zoo.

It was a *Twilight Zone* episode, paths curving off into the fog, empty cages and a few full ones. I didn't like it, I didn't like chasing her alone.

Then it occurred to me I didn't really have to. The gunshots probably had attracted some attention. I'd do my best to attract more, even to inspire some action.

"Phoebe!" I yelled.

My voice echoed through the fog.

"Phoebe! I know you're in here. It's no good. The police are surrounding the zoo! You can't get out!"

"Liar!"

The voice came from so nearby, I jumped. My guess that she probably had no bullets left became a fierce hope.

"I've never lied to you yet," I lied. "You've done nothing but lie to me." It wasn't necessary to yell now, and we both knew it.

"If the police were here," she said, "they wouldn't have let you in here."

"Sure they would. You're out of bullets, so you're no real danger to me. And they think the fact that we're sort of friends might make it possible to bring you in without anybody being hurt.

"Besides, you're a lousy shot. You must have been right next to Winston when you blasted him. You paid him off, right? Then he got a big grin on his face and came to collect another installment of his fringe benefit—namely, your small but perfectly formed self.

"But however fond of him you might have been—I don't know, you might have been just using him—you couldn't have him around as a potential blackmailer. You pulled out one of the guns he got you, punched his ticket, and took the money back."

"Don't you call yourself my friend!" she said. "You rejected me!"

"Well, hell, Phoebe, I'm not the only one. You never got close to Aliou, did you?"

"I never met Aliou."

"True. You learned about him via Weiskopf. But somebody else rejected you, too."

"Who?" she demanded.

"Your husband," I said. "When I talked to him, he not only assumed I was shtupping you, he practically threatened to force me into it at gunpoint."

"Stephen loves me!"

"Of course he does," I said. "To the extent he can love anything."

"Stephen is a great artist!" She was really furious.

"Sure he is," I conceded. I began to inch closer to the sound of her voice. "Is that what this is all about? You were going to steal the company for Stephen?"

"Steal it? How can I steal what's already his?"

She had a good point. Stephen already owned most of the stock involved. What the problem was was *cash*.

"We were doing fine," Phoebe said. "We had the dividends, and we had our investment in the school."

"The visa mill."

Phoebe was scornful. "Who cares about that? It was profitable, and we were doing fine."

"You keep saying 'we.' Was Stephen in on this, too?"

"No! Of course not. The whole idea was to keep him from worrying, so he could devote himself to his work."

No wonder he'd been bewildered at my mention of guns. It was very tempting at this point to yell "His work is *doo-doo!*" but I didn't.

Phoebe's voice dropped. "I—I've left Stephen a letter. I wrote it long ago. It's in our safe at home."

"Why leave him a letter?" I said. "Come back with me and tell him yourself. Nobody's going to hurt you."

"I can't do that," she said sadly. "Stephen will be quite cross with me."

I thought it was more to the point that Lady Arking and the Department of Public Prosecutions might be cross with her, but I was willing to let her go where she wanted to go.

"Stephen loves you," I told her. "You said so yourself. He'll forgive you."

"No." Her voice was heavy with sadness, and quieter all the time. I had to keep inching forward just to hear her.

"No," she said again. "I was planning the one thing he could never forgive. After Pamela was dead, I was going to make him accept the title and salary of Managing Director of BIC. He wouldn't have to do the work. There was a competent person to do the work. It was the title, and the prestige, and the money. The money. We'd never need to worry about money again, and Stephen could fulfill all his dreams and write his masterpieces in comfort."

It just went to show, I reflected, that relativity really worked. If the block of stock Sir Richard left Stephen paid off at less than a million and a half pounds sterling per annum, I was a ring-tailed baboon. Most people would probably consider that comfortable, but geniuses, you see, need much, much more.

"But Pamela was so *mean*. She would never give Stephen anything other than his dividends. She forced me into partnership with Weiskopf. If it weren't for her, I wouldn't have done anything but sleep with him.

"But that wasn't enough for her, was it? She had to go and send her reporters around and ruin the whole business. Then Weiskopf wrote the letter, and she sent that Aliou around, and he found out something. He rang me on the phone and asked me if I knew anything about the school."

"I see."

There were lots of ways it could have happened. Aliou probably made the opportunity for a quick tiptoe through the files and saw a name or a phone number or an address that was worth following up on, and which led him to the opinion that a talk with Phoebe was called for. It couldn't have been anything certain, or he would have had more than just a brochure in that envelope.

Still, it was too much for Phoebe to risk. Indulging her taste for rough trade (she'd made a play for me, hadn't she?), she paid Winston with cash and physical fringes to pull the trigger on Aliou at our rendezvous.

She probably got that out of Lady Arking during a neck rub or something.

"She forced me into it, you know," Phoebe said. "I didn't want to kill anybody, even her."

"Why did Weiskopf send the letter?" As far as I was concerned, that was still the unanswerable question.

She said, with true anguish, "I don't *know!* He must have been insane. That afternoon, all I'd intended to do was seduce you. You'll regret it until your dying day that I didn't. Roxanne may be rich, but isn't she a bit common?

"I'm sorry, there was no reason to hurt your feelings. But I'd planned such a pleasant afternoon, and then you said you were going back to that wretched school."

"And you played Shirley Temple, and cajoled me into taking you along, right? And you had the gun in your purse. And we'd walk into the office, Weiskopf would recognize you, and you'd take out the gun and slaughter us both, right?"

She was petulant. "You talk as if I would have had a choice. I've been *forced* into all this. It's been hell."

"Don't just tell me," I said. "Come back and tell everybody."

"Oh, Matt, I wish I could. And I'm glad it worked out that I didn't have to kill you. Even if you did wind up destroying me. I hope you believe that."

"Sure," I said.

I was taking her with a large load of salt. Now I know why she crept up the stairs that day—so she could listen to our conversation and decide if she still needed to plug us.

"Tell me one thing. Did you trip Weiskopf into the traffic?"

"A little," she said. "Matt, you're getting too close to me."

"I'm just going to take you back to the house," I said. "You can talk to people there."

"They'll put me in jail. There are evil women in jail. They'll want to touch me. I won't go."

"I think," I began. "I can't make any promises, but I *think*, that you'll probably go to hospital, rather than to jail."

"Do you really think so?"

"Yes, I do." I didn't know if I thought so or not. I just wanted to get the hell out of the fog.

"I shouldn't mind being in hospital quite as much," she said. She sounded like a little girl. "I have been so dreadfully tired lately."

I personally couldn't see how she could be, with all the time she spent in bed.

"All right, then," I said. "Then just come along with me and we'll see if we can't get that arranged, what do you say?"

She didn't say anything, not for a long time. I kept quiet, giving her a chance to make up her mind. I was fairly confident that I'd be able to hear her if she ran away.

Slowly, I walked toward the spot her voice had come from. I wanted to be close enough to grab her if she did decide to run.

I got close enough so that she began to take shape. I couldn't make out a distinct image, just a smear of orange and pink in the white air.

I held out my hand. "Come on, Phoebe." I held up my hand. "Let's go on back. It's cold."

I don't know if she took a step toward me before it happened, or if she ever would have. I just know that behind me, a loud, gruff voice said, "What the bloody 'ell are you two doin' 'ere, then?"

A zoo guard. Armed with a rifle. Phoebe screamed and ran.

Animals voiced discontent all around us. I had the presence of mind to yell, "Police, don't shoot!" and took off after her. The zoo guard, in turn, took off after me.

She used her last bullet. I found out later she used it to shoot the lock off another gate. Maybe, in her myopia, she thought it was the fence to the outside. Maybe she just thought of it as a place to hide.

What it was was the gate that surrounded the little grotto that housed one of the animals the zoo had that liked to be out on a cold night. I remembered as soon as I heard its roar.

The Siberian tiger.

## 22

### "Case solved!"

Rory Bremner
*Rory Bremner, Who Else?*, Channel Four

You may be wondering why you never read about these details in the newspaper. After all, MEDIA EXEC'S NYMPHO DAUGHTER-IN-LAW KILLS THREE, GETS EATEN BY TIGER is a story that catches the eye. Even *The New York Times* would cover that, though they'd manage to stick a dull headline on it.

There were a couple of reasons. I discussed them the next morning with Rox.

She was being cynical, you see. Her outlook had been shaped by her own none-too-good experience with media-conglomerate power struggles.

"So the whole thing gets swept under the rug," she said. "Typical."

I could see that this was supposed to be a serious discussion, so I reached out and pulled the sheet farther up her body to avoid distractions. That particular gambit always makes her laugh at me, but as I tell her, Man is not made of wood.

Life would be so much less complicated if we were.

"It's not all going to be swept under the rug. Just the part about her trying to take over BIC as a source of cash for Stephen and his Muse. There isn't any goddamn evidence, anyway."

"What happened to the letter she wrote to Stephen?"

"It was there, all right. It was just heavy on apology and light on detail. Incidentally, that safe held five more guns. She must have had Winston feeling like Guns 'Я' Us."

"How did she meet people like that?"

"She went looking for them. That was in the letter."

"I'm almost sorry I went with Lady Arking to the hospital."

"She asked for you. Besides, Bristow never would have let you see the letter, anyway. He was fit to bust. I think he's going to go get his nose sewn up for the duration of our stay here.

"Anyway," I went on, "Phoebe went looking for thugs and weirdos like Winston and Weiskopf, because, and I quote, 'I was seeking physical stimulation only; mentally and spiritually, compared to you, dear Stephen, men are mindless and soulless blobs.'"

"Wow," Roxanne said.

"Yeah, the whole thing was like that. When I read her writing style, I could finally understand why she liked Stephen's poetry."

"Hey, she propositioned *you,* didn't she?"

"Yep," I said. "One soulless and mindless blob at your service."

"Oh, Matt, if she only knew."

"Thank you," I said. I kissed her on the forehead. Chastely, because the conversation wasn't over, and Man was still not made of wood.

"Bristow is going to close the case quietly, because that's really all he can do. The only one who gets completely protected is the tiger."

"The *tiger?*"

"Yeah, the tiger. By British law, an animal who kills a human has to be destroyed."

"Yes?"

"Do you know how many Siberian white tigers are left in the world?"

"Not a lot?"

"Fewer than that. Besides, it's not like the tiger actually *ate* her. He was sleeping peacefully, minding his own business, when Phoebe shot the lock off, stepped through the gate, fell down the gully, and landed on top of him. Naturally, this startled him."

"Naturally."

"And he lashed out with a paw, like any kitty-cat would. Of course, this particular paw was like a baseball bat with four-inch spikes driven through it. A couple of swipes with that . . ."

"Ugh. You don't have to describe it, I can imagine."

"I don't have to imagine, I saw it. In any case, since the tiger was only acting in self-defense, we're all going to lie to save it. The official story is Phoebe fell down and broke her neck."

"But what about the body?"

"Closed-coffin cremation. This afternoon. We are, believe it or not, invited. Wanna go?"

"You're sick, Cobb."

"I already gave Stephen our regrets, though that doesn't seem to be exactly the right word, does it?

"But as I was saying, the zookeeper loves that cat, he'll personally see that no traces of bloodstained organdy remain? Chiffon?"

"Organdy."

"What's the difference, anyway?"

"Organdy is stiffer."

"Oh. No wonder she wore it. He'll personally remove any trace from the tiger's claws and burn it."

"Better him than me."

"My sentiments exactly. What time is it?"

She climbed up and put her chin on my shoulder to see the clock behind me.

"Ten after eleven," she said. "Why?"

*Killed in the Fog* **213**

"Bernard Levering is picking me up at one o'clock. With Lady Arking recuperating, he'll pretty much be running TVStrato by himself. I thought I ought to have a talk with him."

"If you let yourself get involved in the TV business again, I'll strangle you myself."

"No chance, darling," I told her.

"After this, it's over."

"Yeah," I said. "It's over."

"Then we can probably figure out a way to fill the time between now and the time Bernard shows up."

"I'd like that, Rox. I really would."

"Oooo, so serious all of a sudden."

"You've got to be serious about the important things. At least every once in a while."

"Okay, Cobb," she said. "I seriously love you."

"I seriously love you, too."

My hair was still wet from the shower when Bernard picked me up. He was, he told me, taking the day off from work, but he was dressed for the office anyway. I had on a turtleneck and a denim jacket and jeans.

He drove up in a dark blue Mercedes with a chamois interior.

I got in, buckled up, and asked him if he was hungry.

"Not very," he said.

"Good," I said. "I'm tired of business lunches. Let's drive around a little and see how we feel."

The first place I made him take me was a bookstore called The Lighter Side, on the Upper Richmond Road in East Sheen. The places deals exclusively in comedy books and tapes, and contains stuff you can't find anywhere else. It also serves as a sort of clearing house for a lot of comedians in London.

I bought a couple of comic collections, *Beau Peep* and *Alex*, which are by far the best comic strips in Britain. Bernard waited patiently, though he seemed puzzled.

We left the shop, got back in the car. I suggested we go down by the river. He shrugged and said okay.

We parked down by the terrace in my part of Barnes. "Let's take a walk," I told him.

It was a cool day, probably as cold as last night, but less penetrating than the fog. It was clear, and the usually black Thames reflected a bright blue sky and white clouds. There was a bench a little way along. I sat, and waited for him to join me.

"If you don't mind my saying so, old friend, you're acting rather strangely."

"I've got a problem."

"Maybe I can help," he said. "Lord knows we owe you one."

"You and Lady Arking, you mean?"

"The whole bloody company, Matt. You know that. If you don't, I'm telling you now. Stephen in charge of British International Communications would have been a bloody catastrophe."

"Well," I said, "maybe you can help, at that."

"I'm willing to try. What's the problem?"

"Phoebe. Isn't it always?"

"Whatever she did, she sure paid for." He shuddered.

"I suppose so. It's a pity."

"I didn't know you cared about her to that extent."

"I don't. I'm not getting sentimental over a psycho killer—I'm lamenting the fact that she checked out before all the questions were answered."

"Like what?"

"Well, how it worked out that Winston happened to keep the same appointment with Aliou that I did. How Weiskopf knew I was coming to visit him. Or the biggest question of all: *Why did Weiskopf send that anonymous letter?*"

Bernard scratched his chin.

"When you string them out like that, they do seem hard to figure. Probably coincidence."

I shook my head.

"Nah. It's when you string them out like that that you can begin to make sense of them.

"Take the anonymous letter, for instance. It wasn't just threatening, it was *hurt*. It was *outraged*. This guy's warped but real sense of fair play had been violated. And that could only happen if he legitimately thought that the money for the diploma mill really did come from Lady Arking."

Bernard shrugged. "Maybe Phoebe told him it did."

I nodded. "That's way I read it. Until last night, in the zoo. I asked Phoebe the same question, and she was in absolute despair. That letter started the chain reaction that crashed her whole life. She had no idea what might have inspired it."

Bernard shook his head.

"Then I'm stuck."

"You sure are. Old friend."

"What do you mean?"

"I mean, who knew everything that was going on at TVStrato? Who was routinely apprised of everything Lady Arking did? Who besides Phoebe was the only person I spoke to about my intention to drop in on Weiskopf? And was the only person besides Phoebe who could plausibly represent the money as coming from Lady Arking?"

"Stephen, for one."

"Come off it. Stephen didn't know a thing about my visit to Weiskopf. For another thing, Phoebe died because she was obsessed about how Stephen would react when he found out all of this. No, old friend, no matter how I turn it over in my mind, the answer to those questions always has your name in it. How was she in bed?"

"Do you honestly expect me to answer a question like that?"

"Why not?" I said. "I'm not a cop, I'm not wired for sound, I'm just curious."

He managed a crooked smile. "I'll bet you're curious."

"I'd like to think," I said, "that it was incredibly great, historically great, so great you lost your head. Then, at least, you'd have that much of an excuse."

Bernard looked at the river and mumbled something.

"What?"

"I said she was fantastic!" he said. He turned toward me and leaned in to me. His face was a bizarre combination of anguish and triumph.

"Matt, she was unbelievable, she was like a tornado. She was like a drug. I couldn't stop. I knew about all the other men, I couldn't stop. I didn't love her—I didn't even much like her. But I did what she asked. Yes, I did what she asked. Not that she asked that much."

"But she asked you to arrange the deal with Weiskopf."

"She said she had . . . ah . . . no head for business."

"Did you have a cut of the visa mill?"

"She wanted to cut me in, but I refused."

"Mr. Nobility, all of a sudden."

"I won't even try that one, Matt. Nobility had nothing to do with it. From my point of view, the return was too small for the risk. I'm—I *was* in a fair way to take over as managing director when her ladyship retires."

"Uh huh. Of course, Phoebe did sort of mention you, last night. She said there was someone competent to run the business for Stephen if he took over. He'd have the title, but you'd no doubt have a hefty pay raise to go along with the actual power—you could settle for that, I guess."

"What can I say?" he asked.

"You're doing fine. I suppose Phoebe also asked you to keep her informed of anything her stepmother-in-law was up to. So you more or less fingered Aliou for her."

"I had no *idea* he was going to be shot. Besides, at the time it actually happened, Phoebe was with—with me."

"You don't deserve Sandy, you know that, don't you, you bastard?"

"My hand on my heart, I'm going to from now on. Whatever happens as far as the job goes, I'll make it up to her."

"I believe you will," I said.

"I swear it on my life. Does she have to know about it?"

"That'll be up to you," I said.

"Matt, you won't regret it."

"I'm trying to believe that, Bernard, I really am. There's just one thing that gets in the way."

"What's that?" he said. His voice promised sloppily to remove all my doubts.

"The fact that you tipped off Weiskopf I was coming. What was the idea? For me to kill him, or for him to kill me? Or did you give a damn? I think you didn't care, but I'll never forget that *he* was the one you gave the advantage to."

Bernard had this look on his face. It was a mute question: *How can you make me go through this agony?* I looked away, not because he engendered in me any guilt or sympathy, but because looking at it made me want to drag him the thirty yards to the river and drown him.

"What could I *do?*" he whined. "I was trapped."

"Son, you don't know 'trapped.' You are about to learn."

"What do you mean?"

"I mean a catastrophe is about to befall you. Your wishes are about to come true."

"I still don't get it, Matt."

"Wait for it," I told him. "Bernard, what can I do with you? Can't have you prosecuted, because you haven't actually committed any *crime.*"

I think for the first time I really shocked him. If his conscience had enough life in it that it convinced him he *had* committed crimes, there was hope for him yet.

"You're a treacherous son of a bitch, but if there were laws against that, all the governments and half the businesses in the world would have to shut down. I could get you fired, but what good would that do? You'd just go to work for somebody else. Not only are you a very talented TV executive, you'd know things about TVStrato that could be used against it. And I have a financial stake in TVStrato, through my Network stock. The one thing I can do is destroy your marriage."

"Oh Christ, Matt, don't."

"I said that's up to you."

"How?"

"You are going to run TVStrato, as planned. I think Lady Arking even has it in mind to put you on the board of BIC. You'll take the jobs. And you will do them very, very well."

"I won't let you down, Matt."

"Shut up, Bernard. Leave me out of this. You and I are through. After this little talk, I hope never to see or speak to you again. Got that?"

"I—I understand how you feel."

"Not unless the sight of your own face makes you want to throw up. That's why I made you take me to The Lighter Side. After this, I'm going to need a laugh." I took a deep breath. "You'll do the jobs and TVStrato will prosper. I'll have my eye on you—from a distance. If you screw up, the letters I stayed up all last night writing go out. There are a lot of them. To Lady Arking, to Bristow, the papers, and to Sandy. All the mess I've been trying to avoid will land on you then.

"It'll land on you lots of ways. If anything happens to me, for instance. Or Roxanne. Or anyone close to me. If a competitor is suddenly too smart in anticipating the company's moves. If Sandy lives a life anything short of total happiness. You starting to get the idea?"

He swallowed. "You're making it very clear."

"Good," I said. "Incidentally, Lady Arking is starting the Joseph Aliou Scholarship Fund, for aspiring Third World journalists. You are going to be a major contributor and a tireless worker in the good cause.

"You know, Bernard, you are so much luckier than you deserve, you should be on the cover of the Guinness Book. If you keep your nose clean and do a good job, you'll wind up Sir Bernard in the end. You and I will be the only ones to know what a cowardly scumbag you actually are, and I'll be the only one who ever cared."

He opened his mouth as if to say something, saw my eyes, and closed it again.

I got up from the bench and walked home to Roxanne.

# 23

**"So it's good night from me."**

**"And it's good night from him."**

Ronnie Corbett and Ronnie Barker
*The Two Ronnies*, BBC

*T*he moral of the story is—" I began.

"Stay the hell away from television," Roxanne told me.

"No, the moral of the story is, you can run away from your problems, but wherever you wind up, there'll be a new set waiting for you."

"Is this a pitch to go back to New York?"

"Of course not. That would just be running back to the problems we ran away from in the first place. Besides, Spot is going to be out of quarantine before too long."

Roxanne was in her historian suit; another conference on England's involvement in the American Civil War.

"How do I look?" she asked.

"I thought you didn't ask me questions like that."

"This is business."

I figured out what she had in mind. "Just great enough to wow them without stepping over into frivolity."

She grinned. "I love you," she said.

"I love you, too."

"What are you going to do today?"

"I thought I'd head on down to Brixton."

*"Brixton?"*

"Yeah. I thought I'd find out who owns that basketball court. Maybe we can put it in shape, and start a program for the kids down there. That Thomas could be a player."

"Sounds like a brilliant idea," she said.

"Yeah, better to light a candle and so on. Maybe we can limit the supply of Winstons."

"I wasn't talking about them, I was talking about you. I should have known better than to think you could adapt to a life of leisure."

"I'll get there."

"I hope I live to see it. Got to go." She kissed me, gathered up her briefcase and left.

A little while later, I left, too. As I headed for the bus stop, I was realizing I had it wrong. I'd spotted Christieland, but I'd missed the subtler delusion of Cobbland. London wasn't a backdrop for my personal life, it was the arena for *ten million* personal lives. There was bound to be some friction. All you could do was try to slide through it as smoothly and helpfully as you could.

The bus came. I went off to spread the gospel of hoops to a new land.